The Trail of the Silver Horseshoes

The Trail of the Silver Horseshoes

Stories of the American West

Jiri Cernik

Sunstone Press
SANTA FE

Sunstone books may be purchased for educational, business, or sales promotional use.
For information please write: Special Markets Department, Sunstone Press,
P.O. Box 2321, Santa Fe, New Mexico 87504-2321.

Book and cover design › Vicki Ahl
Body typeface › Chaparral Pro
Printed on acid-free paper
∞
eBook 978-1-61139-402-3

Library of Congress Cataloging-in-Publication Data
Cernik, Jiri, 1942-
[Short stories. Selections]
The trail of the silver horseshoes : stories of the american west / by Jiri Cernik.
pages cm
ISBN 978-1-63293-082-8 (softcover : alk. paper)
1. Western stories. I. Title.
PS3603.E746A6 2015
813'.6--dc23

2015026201

Sunstone Press is committed to minimizing our environmental impact on the planet. The paper used in this book is from
responsibly managed forests. Our printer has received Chain of Custody (CoC) certification from: The Forest Stewardship Council™
(FSC®), Programme for the Endorsement of Forest Certification™ (PEFC™), and The Sustainable Forestry Initiative® (SFI®).

The FSC® Council is a non-profit organization, promoting the environmentally appropriate, socially beneficial and economically
viable management of the world's forests. FSC® certification is recognized internationally as a rigorous environmental and social
standard for responsible forest management.

WWW.SUNSTONEPRESS.COM
SUNSTONE PRESS / POST OFFICE BOX 2321 / SANTA FE, NM 87504-2321 /USA
(505) 988-4418 / ORDERS ONLY (800) 243-5644 / FAX (505) 988-1025

To My Wife

Contents

Preface

"Go West, Young Man." This memorable slogan from the American post-Civil war period propagated by the popular journalist and politician Horace Greeley was met with a great response by thousands of young, and not so young, people in the Eastern United States. The mountainous region between the prairie and the Pacific Ocean attracted people with the luring voice of a siren and promised satisfaction for many aspirations. And it promised not only a possibility to get rich quickly and an unforgettable adventure, but the realization of the most fantastic of dreams.

Jobs for the unemployed, land for the landless and unlimited business opportunities to unsuccessful businessmen seemed just within reach. Gold and silver in the mountains were allegedly waiting only for the pick and shovel of a diligent prospector, and on the large pastures stretching all the way to the horizon, herds consisting of thousands of cattle could graze. With this optimistic vision in their hearts, the native born Americans as well as recent immigrants from overseas gradually settled the West Coast that is today's California, Oregon and Washington, then territories along the eastern foothills of the Rockies, today's Colorado, Utah, Wyoming, Idaho and Montana, and finally the arid Southwest, that is now Nevada, Arizona and New Mexico.

This period which lasted perhaps only thirty or forty years is known in American history as the period of the Wild West. It became known for unprecedented success stories on one hand and harsh reality on the other—destruction of naïve dreams and in many cases unparalleled suffering. Many individuals became overnight millionaires, but others lost their last dollar and many paid for an attempt to realize their visions with their own life. To this period, or perhaps to these people who made it great, were dedicated the stories published for the first time in the Czech Republic by a Western oriented magazine *RODOKAPS* in 1999.

The main reason I wrote these stories was to rectify the significantly twisted view of the American West by Czech readers who are primarily influenced by dime novels and of course by the "Great Myth" created by Hollywood. Film and television contributed tremendously to popularization of this part of the United States and its history, but unfortunately the images they created are quite often a far cry from reality. It is true that dramatic scenes fascinate and attract, but the point I tried to make was that the center of gravity of the drama connected with the life in the American West lay in quite different situations than in the shootouts in the saloons or in fighting with bandits. Yes, many people lost their lives in this way, but many more died in primitive mines when the timber collapsed or because of improper use of dynamite or when they ran out of food or during epidemics of yellow fever, cholera or dysentery during the harsh winter.

Of course many settlers were killed by Indians who resisted the flood of white intruders. Based on estimates, about 20,000 people died between 1840 and 1865 on the Oregon trail which was 2,000 miles long. In practical terms it means that every tenth member of a wagon train did not reach the "Promised Land." Unknown is the number of cowboys who died during roundups when their horses slipped, fell and crushed the riders, or died during summer storms when cattle stampeded and stomped to death the rider as well as his horse if it got in its way.

In other words, if one gets more acquainted with the history of this region, one will see that it is not only the natural beauty which made it famous but also the everyday human drama which occurred at any place touched by the flow of emigrants. One only has to stop at any cemetery in old mining towns or camps like Telluride or Silverton in Colorado or simply any cemetery dating back to the second half of the nineteenth century. Grave stones covered with moss usually indicate medium or young age and the cause of death unromantic. One can say without much exaggerating that probably a sizable number of people who lost their lives during the process of settling the West are buried in unknown places without a grave stone or a cross, but simply in unmarked graves.

The expansion across the Mississippi River toward the Pacific Ocean can be divided into two very different periods: before the Civil War and after the Civil War. The traditionalists and romantics believe that the West before the war was not only a pristine land but also that the handful of whites who lived there were mostly honest people with high moral standards. Actually, they were mainly trappers who lived by their own laws, any visitor was welcome, the log houses were not locked while their owners were on a trapping expedition, a man's word was not to be broken, and a man's honor was worth dying for.

Trappers often married Indian women and the eagerness of young Indian warriors to fight was usually aimed more toward another Indian tribe rather than against the white people. The number of the whites was miniscule and the indigenous population viewed them rather with curiosity than with the feeling of being threatened. Moreover the trappers, who spoke the language of one or two Indian tribes, fully respected the Indian culture and did not occupy any more land than necessary for simple living.

The flow of the emigrants who only wanted to farm or raise cattle was relatively small and was limited primarily to Oregon (Willamette Valley) and California. The vast territories of Montana, Wyoming, Utah, Colorado and possibly New Mexico were not suitable for agriculture and served only as transit regions.

After the Civil War, the situation dramatically changed. News spread that the mountains of the West were rich in precious metals such as gold and silver and that in the eastern sections of Montana, Wyoming and Colorado one could successfully raise cattle. When the Transcontinental Railroad was finished in 1869, the original trickle of white settlers turned into a flood. From the social point of view, the Civil War also had a profound effect on the composition of future emigrants. The war, as any major social catastrophe, uprooted a large quantity of people, particularly in the South. Most of the Southerners were dependent on the work of slaves. These people and their adult children decided to look for their fortune somewhere else and as I mentioned, they positively reacted to the slogan: "Go West, Young Man."

Any war brings undesirable social phenomena such as moral decline, cynicism and depravity and often brings forward certain criminal elements. As a result, the West after the war created the West of saloons, brothels, gamblers, bandits, shootouts, guns-for-hire and general violence, thus coining the new term: The Wild West.

We can safely say that the true villains and the unselfish good guys as depicted by Hollywood movies were in the minority. Most of the new arrivals were just a colorful mixture of people who were looking either for jobs or business opportunities, or immigrants from overseas who believed that the streets in America were paved with gold. They soon found out that it was not true, that in many cases the streets were not paved at all and to their great consternation they learned that they were actually expected to pave them. Needless to say, among these hundreds of thousands of people one could find a number of adventurers, conmen and criminals.

On the whole, however, most of these people were honest, hard working and industrious, but occasionally situations in which they found themselves, and for which they were not always prepared, forced them into actions often contrary to the law or their moral code. This feature becomes apparent in many of the stories I present in this book. One could add that these people were usually individualistic even though leaving home and moving to an unknown country often requires a collective undertaking. So emigrants banded together when their safety was in question such as forming wagon trains to cross the continent or forming a posse to catch the outlaws or organize a militia when there was a threat of an Indian raid. However, once the danger passed, they usually parted ways. It is for this reason that most of the stories in this book bear the name of the central figure, not a group.

These people became heroes in the human dramas that took place all over the American West and which life forced upon them. This is why the stories are not about popularized thugs like Billy the Kid, the James brothers, or Ringo and William Broscius (Curly Bill) of Tombstone, but rather about their victims.

Now, a few words about the creation of the stories. They can be divided into two categories. The first one can be characterized as creative non-fiction, which means that these stories are based on true events but presented in a literary form so they appeal to the reader not only for the plot but also for the character's emotions. These include "Portugee Philips," "Reed," "Jack Slade," "'Soapy' Smith," "Major Wolcott Marches on Buffalo" and "Joseph L. Haywood."

The other stories consist of plots that are fully or partly fictitious, but relate to some historical event such as "Two Jakes" (Gold Rush in Alaska) or a specific place such as "Lulu City" (a ghost town in Colorado). An inseparable part of these narratives are the historical notes at the end of the book which will provide the reader with actual facts and a broader context in which these events took place.

The reader may ask why I wrote these stories. There are perhaps three reasons. One, as a European I was always fascinated with this period of American history. The popular pre-World War II literature available to me with this theme was heavily influenced either by romantic writers like Karl May (a German writer) or simply followed the dime novel model. Two, after arriving in the United States I felt a strong urge to find out "how was it really." My wife and I began regularly visiting the western states and so we had an opportunity not only to see all the historical places but also to gain first hand information about the events that took place there. It was an eye opening experience. The third reason is that I felt I owed this country something for providing me with a new home, the possibility of intellectual growth and the realization of my dreams.

I thought that one way to pay my debt would be to write about this country, and provide Czech readers with information they would otherwise never obtain. After one of the trips along the Pacific Coast I decided to share the impressions about the life stories of the people with whom we Czech-Americans have a lot in common. They were also immigrants. Of course there is no need to emphasize that their lot was much harsher than ours. The reader should gain great respect for these people who often under inhuman conditions, with hardship and everyday drudgery, founded towns, built farms and ranches, pushed railroads and turned wild prairie into fertile fields. Simply, they helped create America in today's size and shape.

The main goal of these stories is to entertain as well as educate the readers and also make them aware of places where these events happened. In case they decide one day to visit the West, there is a greater probability that they will remember the names of these places better after reading this book rather than reading just the travel pamphlets which usually provide information only about the natural sights, accommodation and where to eat, because the dramatic events mentioned in the stories are usually considered only a local affair.

To those who will venture on this great trip and try to get the whole picture, that is to learn also about the fate of these people, I wish "Happy Trails."

In conclusion I would like also to thank also Angela Adams who kept an eye on my English and numerous employees of Visitor's Centers and Park Rangers who provided me with detailed information and a slew of useful materials.

1

Two Jakes

The story I want to tell took place many, many years ago when civilization had conquered the whole north American continent with the exception of one not well known peninsula with a harsh climate. The news about the Klondike gold spread like fire and made people rush there from all corners of the world. Farmers, carpenters, bricklayers, waiters, teachers or cowboys got the gold fever, left their homes, wives and children and rushed headlong into an adventure which if they survived it, marked them for the rest of their lives.

One Jake was born in the Willamette Valley in western Oregon. His mother pulled a plow or a milk wagon and if it was necessary, she also carried on her back Old Bill, owner of a thousand acres of the best bottom land in the area. The local Indians used to say that one day she had saved his life when he had consumed more whisky that he could handle in the "Dirty" Harry Saloon. Harry used to curse and use foul language in such a way that he had no equal far and wide and he fully deserved this nickname. Bill had run into a blizzard on the way home and had made it home safely thanks to that old brown mare. But you know, who would believe the Indians?

His father was a captured and tamed mustang from the Montana Territory. He was like one of those who used to run wild along the Bozeman Trail and quenched their thirst with water from the Little Big Horn. A young Flathead warrior caught him not far away from the reservation. He had fought with him for quite a while before this well-built white and brown Paint got tired and began to respect the rope on his short and powerful neck. When he brought him to the village, all the men came running to see him.

They led the stallion from one teepee to another, praised his head, small ears, and above all, his feet. The hooves were not cracked, as if they were made of steel, the ankles and pasterns were dry without any signs of swelling. Let's pray to the Great Spirit that his foals will be like him, they said. Next spring, the Paint traveled west to the Willamette Valley where the farmers preferred horses with short backs and sloping croups so they could use them under saddle as well in harness.

The moment Old Bill spotted the stallion, he decided to let him mount his mare. He haggled with the stud owner for a while about the fee, but they shook hands for a gallon of aged whisky and eleven months later Jake was born. He inherited his father's build and coloring; only his head and probably his disposition were of his mother. A couple of weeks later he dared to roam away from his dam and when he was six months old, the pasture was not big enough for him. If those ships full of gold had not arrived from St. Michael, Jake would probably never have left the Willamette Valley.

The other Jake was born in Oregon City. His parents came in a covered wagon along the Oregon Trail before the Civil War, but the Indians living near the Willamette River claimed that in the group of immigrants with which his parents traveled they heard a baby crying. But you know who would believe the Indians? Jake always claimed that he had been born in Oregon City and whenever the boys yelled at him that he was a country bumpkin, he got into a fight with them. His dad did not enjoy the new home for long and when he died, his mother buried not only his body, but also the dreams about farming. She tried to make a living any way she could and little Jake helped the local farmers take care of their horses.

Horses became an inseparable part of his life. He used to get up at four in the morning to feed them and water them, and then he brushed them clean and finally put a harness on them so they could be hitched. In the evening he washed them in the creek, then rubbed them dry, fed them and put them in the stable for the night. When occasionally a farmer let him drive a team of horses, they were the happiest days of his life. It did not take long before Jake could drive four horses all the way to Oregon City and return safely without getting in to any trouble. If those ships full of gold had not arrived from St. Michael, Jake would probably never have left the Willamette Valley.

Yeah, the ships full of gold. The first one, the Excelsior, was faster and arrived in San Francisco on July 15th, 1897. The other one, the Portland, which was barely staying afloat, reached Seattle two days later. By that time everybody knew what was in her hold and anybody who had a pair of legs ran to the docks so as not to miss this show. A group of bearded men who were certainly not dressed according to the latest and local fashion slowly walked down the plank. But people could not care less about them.

They came to see what they had brought. And what they had brought, could not be hidden away. A cable from San Francisco did not lie. The sailors were carefully unloading large leather bags and wooden trunks which under normal circumstances could not be that heavy. It took four men to carry just one small bag. The crowd started to cheer. Yes, it's true, there is gold on the Klondike, lots of gold, mountains of gold. All it takes is to hit the ground with a pick and gold will come to the surface. And so that's the way it all started.

In this cheering crowd which carried the Klondike argonauts on the shoulders to the best hotel in Seattle was a middle aged man, about forty years old whom everybody knew as Jake. His friends called him "Jake the Cabbie" because at that time he made his living by driving a cab. The horse and the vehicle belonged to the company for which it charged him ten dollars a day. Whatever he made in addition to it was his but, because Seattle was not exactly the most popular place on the West Coast, the sum he brought home after paying the rental fee was pretty small. Sometime he even did not make those blinking ten dollars. But as to horse flesh, he was known as a real expert, someone who could handle the meanest hard mouth nag. The customers asked him sometimes if he was a native of Seattle, but he used to say that he was born in Oregon City and came to Seattle when the railroad was built. About that time someone told him that he could make pretty good money by driving a cab there, certainly more than he was earning by backbreaking work in the fields or around the draft horses. Jake had a dream like many people at that time. It surely was not a big house in Seattle or even owning a cab company. His dream was much simpler— just couple of hundred acres in the Willamette Valley where he could plow the black soil every spring with a pair of horses. But now, even one hundred acres of good farm land cost a pretty penny.

Jake did not sleep that night. They say mountains of gold. They claim that gold is everywhere. Sometimes all you have to do is just bend and pick up the golden nuggets or loosen the dirt with a pick and grains of gold will glitter in the sun. All he needs is the right equipment, warm clothing and, of course, a pack horse. How would he otherwise get all that stuff to the Klondike and then the bags with gold back to the seashore? No, sir, he could not go there without a horse. Jake fell asleep only toward the morning and when the stars over the West Coast began to disappear from the sky it seemed that they were moving into his eyes.

Three months later Jake was on the ship which had a proud name, the Santa Lucia, and it was heading north along the coast of British Columbia. But let me make perfectly clear that in those days any more or less seaworthy boat headed north. The original name of the Santa Lucia was the Yerba Buena and she was nothing but a creaky freighter hauling coal from Portland and Seattle south to San Francisco. The boiler gave out during her last voyage and when the captain refused to take this leaking wreck of a ship to Skagway, the excited and gold fever possessed argonauts chased him from the ship and found someone else who was willing to take the risk. Coal dust was everywhere, in food, beer, blankets—even in the whisky bottles. On the third day of the trip all passengers looked like an African tribe which had decided to go on a cruise and got lost. The travelers were crowded on the upper deck and their personal possessions were stored in the hold. About two dozen horses and mules shared this space with varied mining equipment such as pans, picks, shovels, ropes and camping gear. These animals suffered most. Not only did the coal dust burn their eyes and irritate their nostrils, but on top of it they were tied next to each other in boxes not more than three feet wide. A sardine can would have been more comfortable than this damn coal tub.

In this dusty hole near the wall stood a broad chested Paint with a short but strong neck and slightly sloping croup. His head was almost all brown, only from the left nostril a narrow white strip stretched toward the middle of his forehead where it turned into a perfect rhomb like star. On his chest and on his back one could see under a thin layer of coal dust evenly distributed patches of white and brown. But most striking were his feet. They were thin with tendons like wires under the skin. While the other four legged fellow passengers restlessly pawed the wooden floor and kept jerking the ropes tied to their halters, the Paint stood quietly as if he knew that it was useless and it wouldn't do any good. Was there not already enough coal dust in the air? So why raise more of it? Well, you guessed right. It surely was Jake the Paint from Willamette Valley.

When one day he took Old Bill in an open wagon to the cemetery, everything was sold in an auction—land, cattle and of course, horses. A horse dealer bought Jake and shipped him straight to Seattle where the gold fever was at its peak and a good horse was worth, well—gold. And when Jake the Cabbie saw him, he did not hesitate a minute. He knew that this horse was ideal for the mountain terrain and if it is true that the blood of a Montana mustang circulates in his veins, then he could not find a horse with more stamina than this one.

The trip to Skagway took almost four weeks. The weather was great, the sea calm and after a foggy day a sunny one always followed. Jake who never traveled further than Seattle watched with amazement the picturesque fjords and endless forests and, by the end of the third week, the rising snow and ice covered mountains of the Yukon Territory. Here he saw for the first time glaciers which glittered in all colors like diamonds set into a bracelet. Every day he used to go into the ship's hold to look at Jake the Paint and during each visit his conscience bothered him. He saw that he begun to suffer like the other horses. His ankles were swelling and he started to cough. Last week two mules died and one large bay had bloody discharge from his nostrils and his cough, caused by the coal dust, was getting worse. Anybody who was a little knowledgeable about horses knew that he would not reach the land alive. But then Jake thought about the golden nuggets, the farm in the Willamette Valley and the stars returned again to his eyes. He turned around and ran to the upper deck and looked longingly at the glaciers which day by day were getting bigger and closer.

Both Jakes disembarked in Skagway around the middle of October. By that time the town looked like the proverbial ant heap. Packs of dogs of different sizes and breeds roamed everywhere and once in a while a mule or a horse broke loose and was racing up the main street with his owner cursing right behind it. Indian packers ran around the piers and with broken English offered their services while dealers with mining equipment fell over each other in praising their goods at "reasonable" prices.

Jake liked this rush and bustling activity. Gold is finally within reach, he thought. But no time can be wasted. It is another four hundred miles along the Yukon River to the Klondike diggings. And if he got delayed and the Yukon froze, he would be stuck in this crazy place till the spring. During the day he purchased some extra supplies and in the evening in a saloon over some genuine rotgut he questioned the Indian guides about the trail. But their answers did not sound encouraging. In order to get to the Yukon, he must cross the coastal mountains to the Bennett Lake and the only way to get there is through the White Pass. There is a trail going through the Pass which was blazed by Captain Moore about the same time when old Cormack was scooping gold rich sand into his pan from the Klondike River. But this cursed trail is passable only at night when it's freezing because it leads through swamps, boulders and mud holes. It also leads over rocky cliffs where it may be only three feet wide and during the day when snow and ice melt not even a mountain sheep would make it. And moreover, the Chilkoot Indians are spreading rumors that they heard an awful noise, horrible rumbling as if huge rocks were falling from the top of the mountains. The Great Spirit is angry that the white men's presence desecrated graves of the brave warriors, but you know, who would believe the Indians? Jake kept twisting and rolling in his tent the whole night. The words of that old Indian did not let him sleep: only at night—three feet wide—not even a mountain sheep would make it.

The next day Jake visited the Paint which he put up in one of the livery stables at the edge of the town. Thanks to the fresh mountain air the cough subsided and only a little bit of dried up coal dust cakes stuck to his nostrils as a reminder of those four weeks spent in the dusty ship's hold. The swelling of his ankles was receding as well and Jake had a good feeling that everything was turning in the right direction. If only the weather would cooperate. Toward the evening he was ready to hit the trail, but the thermometer stopped at forty degrees Fahrenheit and refused to drop any lower. That was not enough. Waiting for the frost Jake spent two more days in Skagway and since the nights were sort of balmy he began to despair.

Finally on the fourth day the mercury dropped to the freezing point. Jake and another fifteen argonauts he met on the ship got tired of waiting and decided to chance it. They couldn't afford to lose any more time because when they get to the lake, they have to build a raft and sail the thirty miles to the mouth of the Yukon River. They have to leave tonight. But the Indian guides refused to go with them. It has to freeze for several days so the trail is reasonably safe. Did gold make them lose their minds? Don't they smell the stench coming from the White Pass? Those are the carcasses of horses which the impatient argonauts drove to Bennett Lake and now they rot along the trail. But the vision of shiny gold waiting for them defied any reasoning. The stars in Jake's eyes lit up and again the thought of the farm land in the Willamette Valley conquered any objections. In spite of all warning sixteen men decided to head that evening for the White Pass.

Shortly after the sunset Jake led the Paint out of the stable, put on the packsaddle and loaded all his prospecting and camping equipment. Then he hung a bag with grain between the pick and the shovel. That's the last grain he will have, Jake thought. Hopefully there will be some on the Klondike. He checked the cinch and the blanket, jerked the rope and began to walk.

But Jake the Paint did not move. He raised his head, breathed in the mountain air and looked at Jake the Cabbie with his large brown eyes as if he were asking him if he knew what he was getting into. "All right, let's go," said Jake, as he jerked the rope again and the Paint slowly followed him. The other argonauts who decided to reach the White Pass tonight camped along the trail and had about a quarter mile head start. After a while the town disappeared in solid darkness. The moon occasionally peeked out of the clouds and apart from the crunching of the freezing snow and tinkling of the packed tools and pots nothing broke the silence.

After about an hour of brusque walking the trail began to slope sharply upward. Based on the information Jake had obtained in the saloon, the easy section of the trail was behind them. Now both Jakes had to slow down. On the right hand side they skirted a rock wall and on the left a black bottomless abyss threatened to swallow them. Here Jake the Paint stopped again. Jake the Cabbie jerked the rope but the horse did not move. "What?" growled Jake. "We can't stand here forever. We can hardly hear those ahead of us." The Paint raised his head, arched his neck and breathed in the wind blowing from the White Pass. His nostrils were wide open, his ears perked up and his head stretched straight forward. But Jake the Cabbie did not have much sense for this kind of behavior. They were on the way to the gold fields, to the Klondike and by morning they have to be behind the White Pass. There is no time for any horse play or theatrics. Stars again appeared in his eyes but they had an evil glow.

Jake raised his hand and did something he was ashamed of from the very bottom of his heart. The whip landed with a sharp crack on horse's rear end. The Paint shook all over his body, but he resumed walking. Jake suddenly felt a gust of warm wind blowing from the East. It was around midnight when he noticed that the snow began to ball up on the Paint's feet. He bent down, cleaned them up and wanted to continue on his way, but Jake the Paint refused to move. "Now what?" Jake grumbled impatiently and pulled the rope. No response. This time the horse that was standing here was not a tame, tractable farm nag that pulled a milk wagon or a plough. This time it was the son of a wild mustang, a mustang that used to run along the Bozeman Trail and drink water from the Little Big

Horn River who stood here like a stone statue. Years of the taming and training experiences had to step aside. Now the instinct of the wild horses developed over centuries and enforced during constant struggle with nature, whose goal was to survive, got the upper hand.

But Jake's goal was different. It was yellow and it glittered. Jake's goal was gold for which one could buy things most mortals could only dream about. Now the bright stars disappeared from Jake's eyes and instead of them little evil fires were glowing. It was not that boy from the Willamette Valley who appreciated horses more than people. It was not Jake the Cabbie who never senselessly hurt a horse. And this strange man, possessed by gold fever, caused Jake to raise his hand with the whip. But Jake the Paint this time did not wait. He reared, tore the rope out of Jakes' hand, turned around and broke into a sharp trot heading back.

Jake the Cabbie froze. Anger, perhaps sorrow, filled his eyes with tears. Jake felt with the pounding of the hooves dying in the distance his gold dream was dying as well. It was moving far away to a place where he could never reach it. Fear suddenly replaced sorrow and anger. The damn beast will break his neck on the next curve. Then he threw up his hands in resignation and set out on the way back. By the crack of dawn he reached the town.

That night an avalanche rolled down the slopes of the White Pass. The Chilkoot Indians claimed that a thirty foot high wall of snow buried fifteen men and ten horses, but you know, who would believe the Indians? And what happened to Jake the Paint? Well, Jake the Cabbie found him in the stable at the edge of town. He stood in a box, looked at Jake the Cabbie with his large brown eyes and the owner of this horse establishment, an Irish fellow with red hair, swore that the spotted critter was smiling.

(Dedicated to the memory of the three thousand horses whose deaths in the White Pass were caused by the Gold Rush during the fall of 1897.)

Historical Notes

The White Pass was discovered by the end of the 1880s by a seafaring captain and trader **William Moore**. W. Moore named the pass in honor of then Canadian Secretary of Interior Sir **Thomas White**, who was in charge of the natural preserves and unsettled territories. W. Moore pushed a trail about forty miles long which stretched from his log house on the coast to Bennett Lake. The log house was located in the area where the town of Skagway was later founded. The trail was passable under normal weather conditions for hikers as well as for a limited amount of pack animals. During the gold rush, however, its passableness got worse. The flood of argonauts caused major erosion and narrowing of an already dangerous trail. The lower part, called **Devil's Hill**, was in some places only three feet wide and a slip of the foot could mean a fall into a precipice several hundred feet deep. The upper part, **Summit Hill**, was formed by a swampy terrain where a treacherous bog could swallow the whole horse including his load. From summer until September 1897 around three thousand horses died here. There were several reasons for this unprecedented massacre. On one hand most of the horses sold to Skagway were not suitable for the mountain terrain and they were often lame so shipping them to Skagway saved them from the slaughterhouse. On the other hand, most of the argonouts had no experience in handling horses including pack animals because they were born and raised in urban areas. As the number of trail users was rising, so was the amount of accidents. Quite often traffic stopped for a long period of time. Poorly packed or overloaded animals then had to stand on one spot, sometimes for several hours, which caused them unbearable pain in their back muscles. Horses and mules crazed by the pain then reared and jumped among the rocks which resulted in breaking their legs and if it happened where the trail was narrow, the fall into the precipice. This irresponsible behavior of the argonauts eventually led to a full closing of the trail by the end of September. In the fall of this year George Brackett, the former mayor of Minneapolis, started to build a road along the mountain slope and its completion in the winter of the same year closed one of the darkest chapters of the Klondike adventure.

Another danger the argonauts had to face were avalanches. The most serious one happened on April 3, 1898 along the Chilkoot Trail leading toward the **Chilkoot Pass**. About seventy people were killed and the bodies were buried at the Slide Cemetery near Dyea.

2

Porlusee Philips

(Based on True Events)

At first glance the Cavalier tavern located in downtown Boston was a pretty quiet place.

A bunch of customers were sitting at a long bar nursing their shots of either whisky, rum, gin or another local or imported beverage while a few oldtimers were napping over a glass of beer. The barkeep made several attempts to persuade them to order a new kind of drink which consisted of several other alcoholic products mixed together, and which was according to the latest fashion called a cocktail, but without much success. However, in another room to the right of the bar, one could hear a cacophony of voices from six men sitting at a big round table. Five of them, based on the way they were dressed and their accent, were undoubtedly local Bostonians who were trying to convince their sixth companion about something.

This man was a little over five feet tall with slightly greying hair, handlebar like mustache which bristled under his nose and a long scar caused probably by a cutting weapon stretched from his left ear over the cheek bone. Judging by the way he talked and his posture one could tell he was a soldier or maybe a veteran. Some of his expressions and a slight accent indicated that he was either born or lived for many years in the West. Suddenly he waved his hand and broke into a loud laughter. "What? Paul Revere and his ride? You must be kiddin' me. All he did, was ride about ten or fifteen miles, until the British caught up with him, cut off his stirrups and sent him home. And you are proud of this? By God, my name is Bill Rogers and I am going to tell you about a ride you've never heard about and probably never will again."

Bill Rogers took a big gulp of Boston beer, wiped off the foam from his mustache and began his narration.

"Well, I guess you've heard about Fort Laramie, haven't you?"

"Of course, that's somewhere in Wyoming along the Oregon trail," remarked one of the listeners.

"That's correct," said Bill and continued. "I served there in eighteen sixty-five with the Second Cavalry regiment. The same regiment which was under the command of George Armstrong Custer during the war. It was not a bad hitch. The trail was pretty quiet 'cause the Sioux moved north of Fort Laramie and we, the horse soldiers, spent most of the time keeping the fort from falling apart and occasionally providing escort for military contractors. Then word got out that gold had been discovered in the Montana Territory. Well, it was not in the same quantity like in California, but there was enough of it that another gold rush was quickly under way. And you can bet your ranch that the Indians were not too happy about this. You see, the problem was that old Bozeman knew quite well that one did not have to travel to the Montana Territory over the Rocky Mountains or North Dakota and so he marched straight north from Fort Laramie along the eastern foothills of the Big Horn mountains. And he couldn't care less that he was traipsing through Indian hunting grounds. Didn't take long, prospectors got wind of this new route and followed in crowds. Now believe me, the Sioux were pretty touchy about this. These hunting grounds were given to them by the Treaty of Laramie and what the hell are them wagons with the pale faces doing there? Red Cloud that was one of their main chiefs, knew damn well, what was going on along the Oregon trail. He knew of all that damage caused by immigrants within the last fifteen or twenty years. You couldn't read about it here in the East, but believe me they overgrazed all land far and wide, brought in all possible diseases and so if it was not enough, they turned the local Indians into a motley bunch of drunks who were hanging along the trail and begged. There is no doubt about it that such a proud Chief like Red Cloud did not intend to tolerate such a mess in his own bailiwick. First he complained, but you know how much attention anybody paid to him. Treaty—shmiety, there is gold in the Montana Territory, the Whites want to mine it, so a bunch of redskins cannot stand in the way of progress. And just so they don't get any wrong ideas, the government ordered another fort built about two hundred fifty miles north of Laramie. It was named Fort Kearny and stood right next to the Bozeman Trail. Well, actually it was not much of a fort, more like a couple of wooden barracks for the officers and enlisted men, a stable for horses and a powder magazine and all of which was surrounded by a high palisade. As luck would have it in the Spring of eighteen sixty-six my batallion was sent to this boonie outpost where at night you can hear coyotes howl and rattlers rattle during the day.

"The fort commander was a certain Colonel Carrington. A sturdy guy, every inch a soldier. He insisted on discipline, but he was not a martinet. Above all, he knew pretty well what he can and cannot do in this by God-foresaken hole while surrounded by several thousand agitated Sioux, Arapaho and Cheyenne. And one more thing: the horses. We enlisted men had to get by with nags provided by the army and they were ornery critters picked from all over the West. But Carrington's mare came all the way from Kentucky. Yes Sir. She was a thoroughbred about seventeen hands tall, pitch black and when Carrington jumped in the saddle, she raised her tail and was highstepping like during a presidential inauguration in Washington. Now the winter was 'round the corner, so the fort needed a steady supply of firewood. Needles to say, thanks to my crummy luck I and bunch of other fellows were selected for this "noble" task. The other boys called us "lumberjacks" and they were not far from the truth. 'Cause to keep the fort garrison warm, you have to keep felling trees almost every other day.

"In the morning on December twenty-first we pulled out of the fort and headed to the nearest woods to cut about three wagons of logs. The forest was not far away, maybe two or three miles, so we hit the road right after breakfast. The unit had about fifty men. Sergeant picked ten boys as guards and the rest of us started to fell one tree after another, cut them in logs, split them and load them. I tell you, we kept moving 'cause it was freezing like hell and the sentinels reported last night that they saw Indians near Lodge Ridge. It was a small hill about half a mile from the spot where we were cutting that cursed firewood. When we had about two wagons loaded, sergeant ordered us to take a break.

"I sat down on a tree trunk a little bit away from the other men, pulled out a flask and took a swig of firewater to stay warm. Holy cow, then it started. The Sioux encircled the whole clearing and because I was closer to them, one of them red devils took a shot at me. Fortunately he didn't hit me, 'cause those guys are never patient enough to aim properly, but give them a bow and arrow and they shoot down a hawk flying over their heads. Well, the break was over, we all ran to the wagons where we had the rifles stacked up and began to fire at anything that moved. About fifteen minutes later the firing stopped. Now what? To hitch the horses and slowly return through the woods would be sheer suicide, 'cause them devils were spread along the road waiting for us. By our estimate there could have been at least two hundred of them. Then sergeant called me and said,

'Rogers, get on the fastest horse and go the fort for reinforcements. Ten men will cover you up through the woods but then in the open you will be on your own. Ride as if the whole hell was on your heels. At the fort you will report what happened. And remember, behind the woods only God can help you.'

"So all I could do was to say, 'Yes, Sir' and mount. Jesus, I was mighty scared. That stretch through the woods was not too long, maybe a half a mile, but during those long five minutes I aged at least ten years. Once the trees were behind me, I thought I made it. I leaned forward, spurred the horse, but that son of a biscuit jumped sidewards...and that saved my life. At that moment I heard the hissing of an arrow and on the left cheek I felt burning pain as if someone touched me with a hot wire. Fortunately the horse finally broke into a gallop and the race for my life was on. The sentinel saw me from a distance and ordered the gate opened. The colonel was told that shots were heard from the direction of the woods and he was already waiting for me. My face was hurting so I could hardly talk, but I gave the report and then went to see the old sawbones to patch me up. Well, what happened next I heard later on from Colonel Carrington and the other officers."

Rogers paused, finished his beer and ordered another one. He also noticed that four other customers who sat at the barn joined the company so they would not miss his story.

"Well, there was no doubt that the 'lumberjacks' needed reinforcements," Rogers continued. "The only question was how many people and who will be the commander. In the end Carrington picked fifty infantrymen from the Eighteenth and thirty cavalrymen from the Second regiments. The command was given to Lieutenant Colonel William Fetterman. Fetterman was an experienced soldier. He fought under General Meade at Gettysburg and as a genuine cavalry officer he was not afraid of anything. If you asked him to bring you a devil, he would haul him all the way from hell and throw in Lucifer as a bonus. But he was a hothead and Indians were sticking to his craw. Moreover, he was supposed to be reassigned back to Laramie and for a soldier like him it was something like an early retirement. He swore that before he goes, he would do his level best to send a bunch of Indians to their eternal hunting grounds.

"Around noon Fetterman and eighty men took off and nobody ever saw them alive again. At first there was no trouble. They rushed to the clearing and chased the Indians away. That was the order. Break up the siege and escort the 'lumberjacks' safely back to the fort. Under any circumstances they were not allowed to approach or cross Lodge Ridge. Well, there was trouble, but of a different kind. The moment the Indians saw Fetterman and his men, they ran and dispersed. For Fetterman, however, who was hell bent to administer proper whipping, or as we used to say to chastise them, this was not much of a fight. And then he spotted a handful of warriors heading up to the top of Lodge Ridge. In spite of strict orders not to go there, Fetterman did not hesitate a second, ordered everyone again to unsheathe the sabers and follow them. When they reached the top, it looked like the fleeing warriors were within the shooting range and so he gave that fateful order to charge them down into the valley. Well, what happened then, nobody of those eighty men had ever a chance to talk about.

"You see, the whole command rode into a trap which was set up by the Sioux Chief Red Cloud. That handful of warriors who were desperately fleeing from Fetterman was just a feint. Their job was to lure the whole unit into the valley below Lodge Ridge where about two thousand Sioux and Cheyenne were waiting. And as soon as they reached the bottom of the valley, their fate was sealed. Red Cloud and Crazy Horse hit them from both sides and in less than half an hour it was all over. When the shooting stopped, we were all waiting for Fetterman and the 'lumberjacks' to show up to give them a festive welcome, but not a soul appeared on the top of Lodge Ridge. When they did not show up toward the evening, we had no doubts. They were either all dead or captured. Of course the second alternative was the worst, 'cause according to the Indian traditions prisoners serve only one purpose—to be tortured.

"The next day Colonel Carrington took one cavalry troop and several wagons and ventured out of the fort to find out what had happened. The situation was grave. He returned in the afternoon with eighty-one mutilated bodies. Not only were they all scalped, but they had their eyes gouged out and ears cut off. Those damn pagans believe that a dead person will sooner or later rise from the grave and they make them permanently blind and deaf so he or she could not harm them. And they do this to all their enemies whether they are red or white. In the evening Colonel Carrington called all of us to the parade grounds. I see it as if were yesterday. On the right there was a big fire burning and on the left next to the palisade stood the wagons with our dead comrades and it started to snow. 'Boys,' he said quite informally because in a situation like this you don't worry much about what the military manual says about addressing enlisted men. 'Boys, there are several thousand Indians out-side the fort and after their yesterday's victory their appetite will get bigger. If Red Cloud decides to attack the fort, without enforcements we won't have a chance. I need a volunteer who would travel to Horse Shoe Creek and send a telegram to Fort Laramie about our critical situation.'

"Well, what am I to tell you. The immediate response was overwhelming silence interrupted only by cracking of the burning pine logs. This was no joking matter because from Kearny to the Horse Shoe Creek it was at least a hundred ninety miles. At that time there was a telegraph station there and later on even stages used to stop there, but at any rate it would be a helluva hike even in the summer, and now it looked like a snow storm was brewing. Moreover there were redskins who could not wait to adorn themselves with a white man's scalp lurking in many gullies along the way. Well, not to prolong the suspense, after a while a short stocky guy stepped forward and said, 'I'll try it.' Now you can imagine what kind of excitement he caused. Who would have the guts or as we say in the West the grit to do something like that. The short guy was a certain John Phillips. We always called him Portugee, 'cause he was from the Azores Islands. He was something like a government contractor. Couple of times a year he and a few other fellas put together a caravan of wagons and traveled to Fort Laramie and then brought back all possible supplies a fort like ours needed. There was no doubt that this man knew the Bozeman Trail like the palm of his hand. In other words, no better qualified individual could have volunteered for this job.

"Colonel Carrington wrote a report for the commander of Fort Laramie, Colonel Palmer, in which he described the current situation and emphasized that an Indian attack could take place at any time and therefore the fort needed help. And then the only thing to do was to pick a right horse and Portugee could be on his way. We were all wondering which one he would choose and believe me it was a hard decision to make 'cause most of those army horses wasn't worth a pitcher of warm spit. Everybody was trying to help expressing his opinion about the horseflesh that would be the best choice but Phillips only calmly packed his things as if he could care less what mount he would ride. And suddenly a churchlike silence fell and one could hear a pin drop. I could not believe my eyes. Old Carrington was bringing his full-blooded mare. He led her slowly to the place where Phillips stood; then he put saddle on her, tied up a grain sack behind the cantle, checked her feet and handed the reins to Portugee. By this time he was all bundled up in a buffalo fur coat and ready to leave. When he mounted, the guards opened the gate, Phillips turned around, grinned and rode out. We all ran up to the ramparts, hoping we may catch a glimpse of him, but the darkness swallowed the horse as well the rider. We slowly returned to the parade grounds.

Nobody talked. My mouth was dry and I had this nagging feeling that nobody would ever see him or the mare alive. By that time the blizzard was raging the full force and even though nobody said anything, at the bottom of our hearts we knew that if those two don't freeze to death, the Indians will get them."

Rogers paused again, took a gulp from the fresh glass of beer and then continued. The number of listeners grew in the meantime by five. "You won't believe me, but that blizzard actually saved our necks. If it were not of that snow storm, we may have wound up like Fetterman. Snow was falling for four days and the thermometer stopped at zero. The snowfall reached about six feet and it looked like the Indians would be able to walk into the fort just over the palisades. But that frost must have cooled them off a little and no warrior showed up in the vicinity of the fort with the exception of a handful of Indian scouts. Finally, about two weeks later the sentinels spotted a dark spot in the distance. It was getting bigger and bigger and then the sergeant started to yell like a maniac, 'Reinforcements! Reinforcements are on the way!' We all ran out and sure enough, there was about three hundred foot soldiers and about fifty cavalry men pushing through snow toward the fort. It took a while before it dawned on us. Jesus Christ, the miracle nobody believed in, actually happened. Portugee obviously made it. You can imagine the joy with which we welcomed those guys. Colonel Carrington was waiting at the gate and as soon as the commanding officer gave his report, we all started asking about Phillips. Only the next day we found out how this historic ride went.

"Well, as I said earlier, Portugee disappeared in the blizzard around the midnight from the twenty-first to twenty-second of December. First he led the horse for about two or three miles and when he believed he had left the Indians safely behind, he climbed in the saddle and galloped south. He rode the whole night. At the crack of dawn he realized that riding during the day would be a risky proposition and so he decided to ride only at night. That first night he traveled about seventy miles, forded the Powder River and before the sunrise, he reached Fort Reno. There he reported what had happened, wolfed down a little bit of food they offered him and because it was still dark, he continued his journey. He did not get a fresh horse. I reckon, when he saw those nags they had available, he had to come to the conclusion that a good tired horse was still a better deal than a lousy rested one. Then he kept alternating between leading and riding the mare, so that she had some rest and at the same he would not lose any time. Around nine he rode into a small canyon ideal for a good nap. He fed the horse a little bit of oats and pulled the coat over his head and went to sleep. He woke up around three in the afternoon, dug himself out of the snow, crunched up a handful of biscuits and fed the mare. The storm subsided, the sun broke through the clouds and when he was ready to mount, he noticed on the opposite canyon wall three shadows resembling horses with riders. There was no doubt in his mind that there were three Indian scouts standing at the edge of the rocky cliffs. Fortunately the snow covered his tracks, so they had no reason to suspect someone down there. Phillips squeezed the mare's nostrils to prevent her from neighing and pulled out his revolver just in case one of them warriors got the wrong idea and rode into the canyon. About an hour later the shadows disappeared and Portugee slowly climbed out of his hideout. There was not a living soul far and wide. Needless to say, he did not linger around. He got back on the horse and hurried away. After midnight the storm returned and he felt his hands and face starting to freeze. He dismounted, tied the reins to his waist and buried his hands under the coat. By walking he warmed himself up a little bit and after a while he resumed riding. However, the mare started to slow down. The deep snow and the headwind took the expected toll on her. The foam around her mouth turned into icicles and it took her longer to catch breath. Phillips knew quite well that if he lost his horse in this kind of weather he and probably the men of Fort Kearny would be past praying for.

"There was still another fifty miles to Horse Shoe Creek and so he decided to take it easy and make it up during the daylight. He was definitely closer to civilization now and the danger of running into the Indians was no longer that great. Toward the morning he reached the Platte River. That night he covered almost a hundred miles, partly because he left before dusk and partly because the ground leveled off. On the bank he tied the mare to a tree and crawled under the nearest bush. This time he fell immediately to sleep. The storm did not weaken and snow kept falling like from a torn featherbed. He woke up some time in the afternoon 'cause he could not breathe. To his surprise he found that he was buried under two feet of snow which actually saved him from freezing to death. He took care of the mare and tried to make fire but no use. The wind was blowing as if it was coming directly from the North Pole and spoiled any effort to lighten up a handful of dry twigs. Well, in the end he gave it up, ate the rest of the biscuits, untied the horse and set out along the bank in an easterly direction. After walking for about two miles he reached a bend where he crossed to other side. But the snow drifts were so deep that he preferred walking on ice which wouldn't break even under troop of cavalry. About two hours later he spotted in the distance a small light—the Horse Shoe Creek telegraph station. If the Virgin Mary accompanied by all of the Saints appeared before the telegraph operator who was that night on duty, he wouldn't be more surprised than when Portugee opened the door and rather fell than walked in. He just wondered what kind of a fool he must have been to try to send a telegram in this foul weather. Couldn't he wait till the morning? But Phillips was so exhausted he could hardly talk. First he drank a cup of hot tea laced generously with rum, then a shot of plain rum on top of it. The operator in the meantime patiently waited to find out what this strange half frozen visitor would come up with. When Portugee finally announced that he had come all the way from the Fort Kearny, he thought he had been joshing and just to be on the safe side he asked him if he actually knew where the Fort Kearny was located.

"Well, Portugee certainly did not feel like joking. He did not say anything, just pulled out of his pocket the Carrington's message and shoved it under his nose. The operator studied it for a while and then sat down and started tapping the text. Now I bet you that you think that Portugee having carried out his order hit a sack near the fireplace and slept like a baby." Fourteen heads readily nodded and one could read in their faces a feeling of great relief that the story came to such a happy end. Rogers smiled, finished his second beer and ordered the third one. Then he snorted and said, "My dear fellows, if that's the case, you are badly mistaken. The operator when he finished sending the telegram, wanted Fort Laramie to confirm that they got it, but the telegraph was silent. Not a tick. Now what? Phillips knew quite well that the Indians often pull down the telegraph poles 'cause they fear the 'witchcraft' of the Pale Faces. Several times they sent their warriors on their fastest horses to deliver a message but the wires always beat them.

"What am I to tell you. Any one of us after having covered one hundred ninety miles in saddle would think twice to walk out again into the raging snow storm and drag his carcass another forty miles through snow covered wilderness. But, as later the telegraph operator said, Portugee scratched his head, stuck the paper with Carrington's message into the pocket and poured himself another glass of rum. Then he shifted from one foot to another and headed out the door. In the stable he rubbed the mare dry, gave her water and oats, but she did not even touch it. It only seemed that she was not breathing as heavily as before. Phillips climbed in the saddle and slowly left the station. Depending on the depth of the snowdrifts they walked either on the ice or the river bank. The storm did not relent and Portugee started to lose feeling in both his legs. He was afraid to dismount and walk 'cause he knew he would never get back in the saddle. Five miles from Laramie the mare fell on her knees and Portugee fell over her head. For a while he was lying in the snow cursing to hell all the Indians in the Wyoming Territory who knocked down the telegraph poles between Horse Shoe Creek and Laramie. The mare got up but was shaking all over her body. Portugee tried to drag himself into the saddle but it was too much for him. He wrapped the reins around his hand and began walking. The mare, with her head touching the ground, followed him. They crossed the river below the stockade. Fortunately the guard had just taken his place above the gate so he was not sleepy. Otherwise they wouldn't find Portugee and his horse frozen stiff until the morning. The mare collapsed in the middle of the parade grounds and several soldiers more likely carried than led Portugee to the officers' barrack. Inside there were festivities in the full swing. It was Christmas Eve and the officers were celebrating with a ball. You can certainly imagine what his appearance did to the Christmas cheer when he stepped in covered with snow, barely alive and with Carrington's message about the demise of eighty-one men in his hand.

Rogers paused to wet his whistle with another beer and then with a broad grin commented: "You seem to be sort of speechless, but I don't blame you. If you kindly consider the fact that Phillips covered two hundred forty miles in three days without warm food and necessary rest, in a blizzard and deadly cold, he didn't get lost and the Indians didn't get him, well, gentlemen, don't take it personally, but what this guy of yours—Paul Revere—did, was just a Sunday ride in the city park. And may lightning strike me if I made anything up, but let me finish. Next day Colonel Palmer signed an order to form the relief column and once the men were organized, equipped and the storm subsided, four companies of foot soldiers and one troop of the Second Cavalry marched out of the fort. When the troop rode along the parade grounds, Lieutenant Colonel Wessels barked—'Eyes Left and Present Arms'—and fifty cavalry men unsheathed their sabers and saluted a black mare covered with freshly fallen snow."

The room fell silent. After a while one of the Bostonians asked, " And what happened to Portugee?"

Rogers smiled and answered, "Well, it almost cost him his life. It took three weeks to heal him, but he managed to escape the Old Reaper. The army rewarded him for his heroic ride quite well and then he bought a ranch and raised cattle. But I almost forgot the most important thing. That telegram never made it."

Historical Notes

John Phillips was born Manuel Felipe Cardoso on April 8, 1832 near the town of Terra on the Island of Pico in the Azores. At the age of 18 he traveled to California to pan for gold. The gold fever brought him to Oregon, Idaho and the Montana Territories and in 1866 to the Big Horn Mountains in today's Wyoming. There at Fort Kearny he found employment as a civilian supplying the fort with drinking water. After the Fetterman disaster he volunteered to carry the message to Fort Laramie. As time passed his historic ride became a legend. Nevertheless some historic facts are important to mention. Phillips did not ride by himself but was accompanied all the way to Horse Shoe Creek by another two men, namely **Daniel Dixon** and **Robert Bailey.** The telegram was sent to the headquarters of the Department of Platte and to Washington, DC, but there was no line to Fort Laramie therefore Phillips had to carry Carrington's message for Colonel Innis Palmer in person. He arrived at the fort at 11 pm on December 25 and he undoubtedly quieted the Christmas festivities. For their heroic deed all men received $300 and Phillips could pick the best horse in Company F of the Second Cavalry. Also, many historians question the story about the thoroughbred from Kentucky. Common sense would dictate that only a tough horse of local breeding, preferably with mustang blood in his veins, would be Phillips' preferred choice. Phillips returned to Fort Kearny in the spring and worked again as a civilian contractor, this time carrying mail. When the fort was abandoned, he moved to Elk Mountain west of today's city of Laramie where he supplied the Union Pacific Railroad with ties. On December 16, 1870 he married Hattie Buck and established a ranch on Chugwater Creek. Eight years later he sold the ranch and moved to Cheyenne where he died November 18, 1883 of nephritis. He is buried in Lakeview Cemetery. His wife Hattie died in 1936 in Los Angeles at the age 94. One can also add that the Indians took revenge for the fact that he enabled the reinforcement of Fort Kearny. In 1871 they attacked the ranch and killed all the cattle. Only after his death did the widow receive compensation in the sum of $5,000. The reader may also be interested to know that Carrington's message survived the ensuing upheavals during the following Indian wars and can be seen today in the National Archive in Washington, DC.

3

Reed

(Based on True Events)

W agons! Wagons of emigrants! Wagons named after the Conestoga Valley in Pennsylvania. Their owners call them "Stogies." Not even five feet wide, twelve feet long and covered by canvas bleached almost white by the burning sun. On each side a wooden barrel of water which with every passing day is running lower and lower. Next to the barrels are mounted axes, saws, picks and shovels. Inside are the most necessary objects for a new beginning in a new land. Pulling the wagons are two or three pairs of oxen which are the only animals capable of tolerating the killing heat and thirst and at the same time able to pull the loaded wagons. If the family is lucky, a spare pair walks behind the wagon. Most of the emigrants, however, lose them along the way.

A man with a long whip walks along a wagon and drives the team. Women and children, if they are healthy, also walk in order not to make the oxen pull unnecessary weight. Their faces reflect exhaustion and apathy. They will keep walking practically all the way to California. In a good terrain they will make fifteen, maybe twenty miles a day but in the mountains only five. They will walk through an inhospitable land without pasture and water for their animals. They will walk through the afternoon heat when the sun will burn their cheeks and cracked lips. They will walk with their heads down and eyes staring at the ruts in the sand or clumps of grass which were cut by the wagons of emigrants passing before them. They will walk along the California Trail to Sutter's Fort eight hundred miles in the distance.

When a particular group of emigrants entered Fort Laramie, it registered as the Donner-Reed Party. Donner was a farmer from Illinois who could not resist the rumors about highly fertile land in the California Valley where wheat can be harvested twice a year. As he was quite well off, most of the members of this party agreed to name it after him. James F. Reed was born in Ireland. Irish blood flowing in his veins was from his mother and the Polish, we can even say aristocratic, from his father. His original name was Reedowski and after his arrival in America he changed it to Reed. In Illinois he got involved in various business ventures but with no great success so he decided to try his luck in new land at the Pacific Ocean. He was actually the true leader of this party and so his name appears right behind Donner's. The whole wagon train consisted of eighty-seven people including women and children and twenty-three wagons. At first glance, the group looked like many others heading west along the Oregon or California trails. However, one feature made it quite different. It left Saint Louis too late. According to the original plan it was supposed to join L.W. Hastings, an experienced guide who traveled to Oregon and California several times, and who after his return published *The Oregon Trail Guide*. The emigrants believed this general narrative about terrain, Indian tribes and life along the trail without any reservations. It was sort of a traveler's bible. Hastings even bragged that he discovered a shortcut for those who were headed to California and this shortcut would save up to four hundred miles. Instead of traveling all the way to Fort Hall, one had to turn south at Fort Bridger, cross the Wasatch Range, then go directly to Salt Lake and there pick up the California Trail. Hastings even promised this group that he would wait for them at Fort Bridger, but when they pulled into the fort, there was only a message for them to take the shortcut and that they would definitely catch up with him along the way. As the party was significantly behind, they unanimously agreed to follow Hastings' instructions even though they would have to travel through unknown terrain without a guide.

They will never, as long as they live, forget the crossing of the Wasatch Range. It was bound to happen. They got lost in the mountains and with unimaginable hardship had to push a new trail. One will not be surprised to hear that when they reached the Salt Lake that instead of running into a waiting Hasting they found his message with superficial and quite imprecise information about the Great Salt Desert stretching in front of them.

Here at the grassy hills along the lake they decided to rest. According to Hastings' message they would now have to cross a desert covered with a thick layer of salt and they would not be able to replenish their water supplies and water the animals for another forty or fifty miles. After having rested for several days they moved out of the camp. On the second day they left the lake behind and looking west they set their eyes on a fantastic sight. Children began to exclaim joyfully, "Look, there is snow there, we'll pick it up and we'll have plenty of water!" Yes, just like frozen snow in the afternoon sun sparkled, with an endless plain of salt crystals, the Great Salt Desert—one of the seven wonders of the American continent. It was fifty miles of blinding white, quivering hot air and frequent mirages. It seemed at the beginning that crossing the salt desert would not be any worse than traveling through other arid areas, but after several days it became apparent that the salt had become their worst enemy. Salt was everywhere. It burned the eyes, burned the skin and made the oxen's feet bleed. Moreover, the thickness of the salty crust varied and often was not strong enough to hold the wagons. The wheels began to break through it and the salty mud kept sticking to the iron tires and oxen's hooves. On the fourth day the situation became critical. The salty dust not only made everybody more thirsty, but the salt had to be washed out of the oxen's feet so they would not go lame and there was no spring or a creek where one could refill the barrels with fresh water. There was no question in anybody's mind that if they don't leave this hell the next day, a catastrophe would be unavoidable. Hastings said it would be fifty miles to a next source of water; well, they covered fifty miles and no water was in sight.

On the fifth day the salt receded and was replaced with plain dirt, but toward the evening the oxen refused to go any further. They were at the end of their strength and did not respond to anything including blows with whips. The only solution seemed to be on the horizon where one could see bluish mountain peaks because that's the place to look for water. The oxen had to be unhitched and driven there. Those who survive this ordeal would be brought back and re-hitched. Reed gave orders to his hired hands, jumped on his thoroughbred grey mare and took off toward the mountains to scout for water. When he returned toward the morning, he saw a frightful sight. Most of his animals had torn loose and, crazed by thirst, headed toward the mountains where they disappeared in the countless canyons and ravines. Donner's family, which was ahead of the others, had better luck. Their people found a small river. It was great news because it was, without any doubt, the Humboldt River. They were back on the California Trail. They were no longer lost. The trail would now follow its river bed and that also meant the end of thirst. The cheerful atmosphere, however, did not last too long. The crossing of the Great Salt Desert cost them half of their animals. In practical terms, it meant they had to abandon many wagons, unload unnecessary items and leave them to their own fate. Several families, including the Donners, left behind four wagons altogether. They loaded the most important items into the remaining wagons and the rest of them they buried along the trail fondly hoping that one day they would come back and reclaim them.

The trail was winding through an inhospitable arid landscape. Dust replaced salt and even though the question of a lack of water was temporarily resolved, a new trouble arose—lack of pasture. Scanty clumps of grass could not provide enough pasture for all animals in spite of their reduced number. In the evening at the campfire they decided to take a drastic but also dangerous step—divide the wagon train into two small groups. The reduced number of wagons made it easier to find suitable pasture and a place to camp. Donner took over the first group and Reed remained with the other. After several days a feeling prevailed that after all the troubles they conquered there was a good chance they would catch up with Hastings. He could not be far away.

The wounds caused by the salt desert were slowly healing and the overall atmosphere was getting better. Both groups were moving on top of a mountain plateau and daily covered over twenty miles. The terrain suddenly changed and with it also the river. Instead of getting wider like any river in its middle part, the Humboldt River actually started disappearing and, in some places, it just turned into several pools of stinking water. The old enemy, the shortage of water, was coming back, but this time accompanied by shortage of food. The emigrants relied heavily on hunting and they drew from their own provisions only in case of emergency.

During the last two weeks, however, they were not able to catch or even shoot a rabbit or a duck, and consequently, their scarce supplies were getting scarcer. Good mood was replaced by nervousness, backbiting and irritability. The heat was not relenting and on top of it, the local Indians began to shadow the caravans, and under the cover of night, drive away a cow or an ox, or if they could not do that, then they at least wounded them with arrows. The first clash among the emigrants took place one afternoon, when a father whose family was without drinking water for two days, asked another man to give him a small cup of water for his children. The man, however, refused even though he had enough water because his family was not that large. Only when he saw a revolver pointed at his chest did he allow the desperate father to scoop the precious liquid from his barrel.

The plateau now changed into a highland through which, from time to time, ran a high mountain range traversing the area from north to south. In order to cross such an obstacle the emigrants had to hitch four to six yokes to one wagon, bring it to the top, and then repeat this task several times, until all wagons were on the other side of the mountain. Needless to say this process was slow, tiresome and demanded a lot of patience. In cases like this the whole caravan covered only several miles a day. Fatigue, thirst and the notion that they were getting again farther behind Hastings drove everybody to the edge. While this state of mind dominated most of the emigrants, another incident took place which permanently tore apart all bonds that had held these people together.

The ruts left by Hastings' wagons led directly to a black rock wall and then to a ravine which was relatively passable, but quite steep. The emigrants started to double or triple their yokes. John Snyder and his family, however, decided not to waste the time. His wagon was not too heavily loaded and his team was strong. He decided to try to reach the top of the ridge with only four oxen. However, in the middle of the slope the animals began to slow down and then, exhausted, they stopped. Snyder realized that he had overplayed his hand. The other wagons with four or five yokes were catching up and finally, because there was no way to pass Snyder, they too stopped. Snyder became desperate. The remarks and comments of his fellow emigrants mentioning irresponsibility and foolishness were ringing in his ears. He did not want to change his team but everyone was now stuck. We'll have to block the wheels of his wagon, unhitch several of our own yokes and hitch them to his wagon. How come he did not think about this down there at the foot of the ridge? Desperate, Snyder raised his rawhide whip and with blow after blow pelted the poor animals. Every crack of the whip left a bleeding wound several inches long. At that moment Reed, who supervised the crossing of the ridge on the other side, appeared at the top of the ravine. He spurred his horse, rode to the standing wagons and rushed toward Snyder, who as if having completely lost his mind, kept whipping the oxen. Reed tried to wrestle the whip out of his hand but Snyder was stronger and suddenly turned the whip and hit Reed with its handle. Pain, blood and unheard of humiliation blinded Reed. He pulled out a long hunting knife and stabbed Snyder. The knife went through Snyder's sweat soaked shirt and because it did not hit any bone, plunged all the way into his chest. Snyder struck Reed once more, knocked him down to his knees, but then he himself collapsed in front of the bloodied oxen. When his family gathered next to him, Snyder was no longer breathing.

In the evening at the campfire the emigrants debated Reed's fate. According to tradition the murderer has to pay for his deed with his own life. Reed was not only a murderer but also an unpopular leader of the caravan. He was unpopular for his aristocratic origin and quite often for his condescending attitude toward the others. In addition, while all emigrants traveled only with oxen, Reed set out on this trip with a thoroughbred mare which was the cause of poorly hidden envy. Her slim legs carried a body sixteen hands tall with a small head and arched neck, but it would not be enough that her name was not Betsy or Jenny, but Glaucus, a Latin name most of the other people did not know how to pronounce. Reed's daughter Virginia did not walk along the wagons like children of all emigrants, but rode her own pony. His wagon! By God, it was the biggest and most comfortable. While the rest of the emigrants had to be satisfied with modest Conestogas, Reed's wagon was custom made and resembled a luxurious hotel on wheels. The situation was serious. Reed did not have many friends and most of the emigrants believed now was the time to cut him down to size. Snyder's widow pulled out the family Bible and started to read aloud the passage which said that eye for eye and tooth for tooth was God's true justice. Keseberg, a German immigrant, raised the tongue of his wagon and fashioned it into a primitive gallows. Keseberg also longed for revenge. It was Reed who, when passing through Wyoming Territory, forced him to return to the Sioux all the objects he stole from an Indian grave.

Thanks only to his two hired hands, Eddy and Elliot, who were armed up to their teeth and the plea of his wife, did the rest of the group agree not to insist on carrying out the verdict. The death sentence was changed to banishment. Reed had to leave his family and ride alone ahead of the wagon train. No one was allowed to contact him and provide any help. He got only his horse and food for three days. Everybody was convinced that if he did not reach Hastings in time, thirst, hunger or Indians would take care of the punishment for them. It would be only a question of time before they found his dead body along the trail. Reed said goodbye to his family and left. The next day he reached the part of the train that was led by Donner and after describing to them the tragic event, he continued on his way west.

Two men. One rides slowly on a grey horse and the other walks next to him. The rider has his head bandaged, apparently from some sort of injury. The walking man carries a backpack and a rifle. Both are covered in grey dust and are tired. After several miles they switch. The man with the backpack climbs in the saddle and the rider walks behind him in small clouds of dust raised by the horse's hooves. They rarely speak as if they were saving their strength. After a while the man on the ground asks the rider if he sees anything. The man in the saddle just shakes his head and then they are again silent. The two men, who are the only sign of life in the entire area, are Reed and Herron.

Herron was one of Reed's hired hands who joined the first group under Donner. He felt that it had been his fault that Reed lost most of his animals and had to abandon two wagons. He believed, in his simplicity, that if he had paid better attention to Reed's oxen, they would not have run away. When Reed reached Donner and Herron heard what happened, he did not hesitate. Now he had an opportunity to undo his mistakes. The next day when Reed saddled up his horse to continue alone his journey, Herron suggested that he should join him. Two of them will have a better chance to survive, especially because Herron had a rifle. Reed gladly accepted.

During the first three days they made almost thirty miles a day. Most of the time they followed the Humboldt River flowing through an undulating terrain and occasionally they came across a grassy area and banks covered with thick reeds. On a spot like that, they even shot a wild goose. The situation got worse, however, when the ruts of Hastings' wagons turned away from the river and pointed north. The greenery along the river gave way to desert, grey rocks and alkali dust. The chance that they could rely on hunting disappeared and they had to draw from their own meager supplies. When they reached the Truckee River, the last of the corn pancakes, sugar and tea was gone and the temperature at night dropped to the freezing point. It was the middle of October and toward the evening one could see snowflakes flying. Then on one sunny day they saw in the distance the majestic beauty of the Sierras' snow covered peaks. Both men then entered a narrow canyon which led to Truckee Lake. At the bottom of their hearts they believed that that's the place where they would find Hastings.

In another two days they barely covered twenty miles. The terrain started to rise sharply and the mare was so exhausted that she could no longer be ridden. The landscape profoundly changed. Tall pines with reddish bark and thick green grass skirted the river and the ground was covered with a mix of moss and brown needles. Reed decided to spend at least one full day in this oasis. The mare would have a chance to graze and hopefully regain her strength so that she would be able to carry a rider again, and most importantly there would be a chance to shoot a rabbit or even a deer. The Sierra foothills, however did not show any signs of life. The game, sensing the coming winter, moved either further south or to the other side of the mountains toward the California Valley. Here Herron mentioned for the first time that they should shoot the mare and in this way secure enough food for crossing the mountains. Reed resolutely rejected this idea. As long as she can walk along, it would be utter nonsense. There is a good chance we'll catch up with Hastings at the lake or we'll have better luck with hunting because the game usually congregates near a large body of water.

The next day the terrain flattened, the forest receded and both man could enjoy a breathtaking view of Truckee Lake lying between two promontories. On the other side of the lake they could clearly distinguish a steep rocky wall interrupted in the middle by a deep gap. This mountain saddle was the last obstacle on their way to California, but Reed and Herron were not particularly inclined to admire the beauty of the Sierras. The last time they had anything to eat was four days ago. They tried to find some forest fruits like blueberries but if there were any, either the wild animals picked them or they just fell to the ground and rotted away. Reed suddenly began yelling and waving his hands—Stop! Wait! On the right hand side of the lake, among the pines he spotted a wagon. The wagon was not moving. When after a while they reached it and caught their breath, they realized that it was one of those wagons which had met the same fate as many of their own. It was abandoned by its owners. Why? Only God knows. Maybe the last yoke of oxen which pulled it had collapsed from exhaustion; maybe the man who lead the team died and no one could take his place. Who knows? The only witnesses—the lake and the red bark pines were silent.

Reed rushed to the wagon and searched every inch of it. Maybe he'd find a pinch of rice or beans, or crumbs of corn pancakes...nothing. Absolutely nothing! Then he saw some black object lying in grass. He dragged it out and was holding in his hand a cooking kettle. He put it on the nearest rock, pulled out his knife and began to scrape its inside walls. During those weeks and months while it was in use, layers of something that could be eaten must have stuck to its inside.

After about half an hour of scraping, he gathered a hand full of brown dusty flakes which he mixed with water. He kneaded it into a small ball and then cut it in half. One half was for him, the other was for Herron. It has to suffice for now. Hopefully we'll find something to eat on the other side of the pass. In the evening they camped on the western side of the lake below the mountain. It was again snowing that night. In the morning, cold and tired after a sleepless night, they set out along a narrow trail winding between large boulders toward the top of the mountain wall. The trail followed a sharp incline and both men had to stop every fifteen minutes to rest. Looking at the trail Reed realized that the wagons pulled by oxen could never make it to the top. The only way to get them there would be with ropes. The oxen have to be unhitched, a spare wheel which would serve as a pulley mounted at a suitable place, and a thick rope tied to an end of the wagon with the other attached to the yoke. Then the oxen would slowly walk down the hill and in this way they would pull the wagon to the top of the pass. Needless to say this process would have to be repeated several times.

It took them several hours to ascend the pass. When they approached the top, there was about a foot of snow lying on the ground. Trees were gone and only large boulders lay scattered on both sides of the trail. To the left they could see a little lake but no sign of Hastings, not a living soul. Only the marks left on the rocks by the iron tires indicated that some time ago a wagon train passed through. The terrain was slowly sloping down and the trail widened and led to a broad strip of pine trees. It was here where Reed and Herron decided to spend another night. They would be protected from the cold wind and God willing they may finally find some game. In the evening at the camp fire Herron again brought up the question of Reed's mare. Climbing up the pass she lost her last shoe. Her hooves were bleeding and she limped. So why prolong it? There was another hundred miles to Sutter's Fort and only God knows where Hastings was. Maybe he and his people were already at the fort, having filled their bellies and housed themselves in dry and warm quarters. We haven't eaten anything for a week except for those stinking scrapings.

Herron evidently coped with hunger much worse than Reed. And he was occasionally delusional. Suddenly he saw a bear in the distance, but when they came closer, it was just a black stump, or he would whisper that there was a deer lying ahead of them, but Reed could tell that it was only a reddish trunk of a pine. Sometimes he was accusing Reed that he had secreted extra food and that he did not want to share it with him. That night Reed did not sleep well. He thought of life in Illinois and in his dreams he saw a young grey filly running in a corral behind the house and when he called, she came trotting to the fence. Then he saw himself on a large grey mare covered with sweat and galloping to town to get a doctor. It happened when Virginia lay feverish in bed and her parents were afraid she would not be alive by the morning. Then again he dreamed that he was returning on the same mare home from a hunt when a pack of wolves got their scent and now was on their heels. The mare with her neck stretched ran like never before because she knew their lives were at stake.

Reed woke up at daybreak. The ground was white, covered with frost and as he tried to awaken Herron, steam was rising from his mouth. Frozen stiff they began to descend into the valley. Reed thought about the dreams from last night and they just strengthened his resolution. No, as long as the mare can walk he will not permit her slaughter. She had crossed with him half of the continent and now when the goal of their journey is within reach, he shouldn't give her up, absolutely not. It's true that she limps, but that's because her feet hurt. Once she is able to rest, the hooves will heal and she will be okay again. Both men were trudging slowly ahead, slightly bent forward like anyone who is trying to suppress pain caused by starvation. Around noon they reached a small clearing. Herron suddenly slowed down. Reed looked back to see what was going on and then he realized that Herron was loading his rifle. Did he really spot an animal or was it another of his hallucinations? Herron stepped closer and looked blankly at Reed. His question, why he loaded the rifle, remained without answer. He slowly raised it and aimed at the horse. The mare as if knowing what was coming and not wanting to make it more difficult for Herron, did not move. Reed rushed in front her and beseeched him not to shoot. Herron hesitated for a second and then aimed at Reed.

The deathly silence was interrupted by cracking of dry branches and then a coarse voice asked a question, "Hey, you two! What are you doing there?" Herron lowered the rifle, turned around and among the pine trees saw a man dressed in a suit made from deer skin and richly decorated with fringes along the sleeves. He was one of the hunters providing fresh meat for Hastings' wagon train which was camped in the same valley about a half mile further west. The ordeal was over.

Two clouds of dust rose about one hundred and fifty miles back east from the spot where Reed and Herron met the Hastings' wagon train. They are about five miles apart and a closer look told that it was the hooves of oxen and wagon wheels of two caravans which raised the dust. A man with a long whip walks along a wagon and drives the team. Women and children if they are healthy, also walk not to make the oxen pull unnecessary weight. Their faces reflect exhaustion and apathy. They will keep walking practically all the way to California. In a good terrain they will make fifteen, maybe twenty miles a day, but in the mountains only five. They walk through an inhospitable land without pasture and water for their draft animals. They walk through the afternoon heat when the sun burns their cheeks and cracked lips. They walk with their heads down and eyes staring at the ruts in the sand or clumps of grass which were cut by the wagons of emigrants passing before them. They walk along the California Trail and they don't know yet that soon they will walk into a trap which the cruel and merciless nature set up for them. They don't know yet that in several weeks they will get snowbound in twenty feet high drifts in the Sierra mountains and that they will spend almost five months starving at the shores of the Truckee Lake, a mere three miles from the pass which opens the way to Sutter's Fort. They don't know yet that half of their fellow emigrants will not survive and the rest will consume the flesh of their bodies in order to live to see spring. Right now they walk with their heads down along the California Trail.

Historical Notes

Reed and Herron joined the Hastings group and after several days arrived safely at Sutter's Fort. Here their paths separated. Herron joined the American colonists who rose against the Mexican government which at that time ruled California. Reed, however, fully appreciated the danger which threatened the emigrants on the other side of the Sierras, namely acute shortage of food, and he tried to obtain extra provisions. After a short stay at the fort he, two white men and several Indians set out east. They drove a herd of mules loaded with food, compliments of **Captain John Sutter**. When they approached the mountain range pass (now **Donner Pass**), they ran into six foot high snow drifts. After several unsuccessful attempts to break through, Reed realized that only a large group of men equipped with snowshoes could overcome this obstacle and he returned to the fort. At the fort he asked John Sutter for help, but there were not enough men available there so Sutter suggested that Reed go to San Jose and contact a military commander for assistance. **Captain Charles M. Weber** readily agreed but because the army badly needed officers, he asked Reed in return to temporarily join the fight. Reed seeing that he did not have any other option accepted and shortly thereafter he took part in the battle of Santa Clara with the rank of Lieutenant.

In the meantime the commander of Fort Sutter **Captain Edward M. Kern**, Sutter and nearby rancher **John Sinclair** organized the first rescue party. A group of fourteen men led by a certain **Aquilla Glover** set out for the mountains on January 31, 1847. This expedition successfully reached the emigrant camp on the right shore of the Truckee Lake (now **Donner Lake**) and brought back twenty-three people including Reed's wife and two children, daughter Virginia and son James.

The conflict between the Mexicans and the Americans was ended by the victory of the American rebels and was later followed by annexation of California to the United States. Reed returned to Sutter's Fort and immediately organized the second expedition consisting of him and ten other men. This group left the fort on February 22, managed to get through the pass and return with seventeen people including his other daughter Martha and son Thomas.

The third rescue party left March 13 under the command of **William H. Eddy**. This group consisted of eight men and brought back six people.

The last expedition lead by **Fallon Le Gros** departed April 13. It consisted of seven men and brought back the last living member of the Donner Party—Lewis Keseberg.

Out of eighty-seven members of the Donner-Reed Party only forty-seven people survived the trip to California. Five of them died along the way from Fort Bridger to Truckee Lake. The tragedy at the lake and attempts to cross the mountains took the lives of thirty-four emigrants. One man died after arrival at Sutter's Fort. Among those who did not survive the stay at the lake were George Donner and his wife Tamsen.

The news about the tragic fate of the Donner-Reed Party shook everybody who was at that time heading to Oregon or California. The tragedy in the Sierras entered the subconscious of the Americans as a symbol of hardship and the sometimes inhuman conditions under which the American West was settled. As a curiosity we can also add that a mere twenty years later when the Transcontinental Railroad was built, it went through the Donner Pass.

4

Jack Slade

(Based on True Events)

An open slope without careful planning or land surveying lies along the main street of a new town. On one side there are two stone buildings, one of which carries a black and white sign proudly announcing that it is the home of The Virginia City Theater and on the other side one can see a long row of wooden buildings covered with rough cut pine weatherboards. The row of houses is occasionally interrupted by a horse corral or a building site where stacks of freshly cut lumber wait to become, later on, another store, hotel or saloon.

It is the year 1864 and the gold mining town of Virginia City is permanently marked on the Montana map. Today the main street is quiet. One cannot hear the sounds of boards being sawed and nailed by carpenters or the chiming of a hammer in the blacksmith's hand shaping new shoes for horses or mules. At first glance, one could even say that the town is abandoned, but this impression would be deceptive. At the end of town below the hill where the main street turns into a broad country road there swells and moves an excited and noisy crowd. Up to one thousand miners digging and panning for gold along Alder Creek and practically all inhabitants of the town are gathered here. The black mass of men, women and children is concentrated around the tall gate of a large cattle corral. Under the top cross beam there is a short stocky guy standing on a wooden box. His hands are tied behind his back and his blue eyes wander restlessly around. It seems he cannot understand what is going on. He hears voices from afar coming from the crowd and then the voice of a man standing next to him. He speaks deliberately, talks about achievements and calls for calm and understanding, but the crowd does not want to listen and responds angrily. "Hang that scoundrel! Don't waste our time! He should have hanged a long time ago! You know how many people he has on his conscience? Any decent person is afraid to leave the house in the evening. Go ahead, hang him! We cannot stand here the whole day!"

The screaming and yelling calms down for a moment and the same man dressed in the black coat spreads his hands and turns toward the gathered miners, "People, be reasonable! Don't you see who you are condemning to death? It's Jack Slade. The same Jack Slade who last year when there was no food in town, drove seven hundred miles to the Milk River and back and brought badly needed provisions. None of you volunteered. You were afraid of the Sioux and Blackfeet. No one dared to leave Alder Creek. Jack was the only one who had the guts to go there. He returned with wagons full of flour and dried meat. Well, he may have consumed a little bit more whisky than he could handle yesterday, but you don't want to hang him like some outlaw who robs stage coaches, do you? Think of his wife Virginia!"

The allusion to Slade's wife had a somewhat calming effect on the rowdy crowd and Judge Davis took advantage of it like a drowning person grasping at straws. "Have you forgotten her charity? Have you forgotten how many people she helped when they were sick and you want to make her a widow?" Several men standing close looked down and indecisively shifted from one foot to another. The judge then leaned to a small boy next to him and whispered something into his ear. The boy nodded, slipped out of the gathering and after a while one could see him galloping out of town toward Meadow Valley. At that moment the man under the cross beam turned toward the judge and finally spoke out, "For God's sake, keep on talking. Don't stop! As long as they are listening, they may relent." Davis wiped the sweat off from his forehead and remarked, "That I know. The question is if they let me talk long enough before Virginia can make it here." The judge straightened up and resumed his plea, "You know what kind of shame will fall on our town when the people of Montana and Wyoming find out that you hanged Jack Slade? Jack Slade who worked for old Ben Holladay? Do you realize what that will mean?" Having heard the name of Ben Holladay the man on the box shivered. His restless eyes looked at the surrounding hills and the judge's voice began to sound distant. Jack Slade's spirit was no longer in Virginia City and he did not see the noisy crowd of miners who wanted to hang him. In his thoughts he returned to Atchison in Kansas where it all had started four years ago.

At that time Jack worked for Ben Holladay as an express man. He was in charge of wagon trains hauling goods from Kansas to Colorado and the military supplies to Fort Laramie in Wyoming. He was reliable. He never lost the freight;

he took good care of the draft animals and treated the wagons as if they were his own. Moreover he always arrived on time. It's true that when the job was done he looked into a bottle of whisky more that he should, but no one held it against people in this profession. You see, to spend weeks and months on the prairie, fighting off Indians, fording rivers and to breathe dust raised by several tens of yokes is certainly no pleasure. So it became more or less a rule that after such a long trip the boys usually painted the town red. So what if Jack Slade added a little bit more red paint to the Silver Horseshoe Saloon in Atchison. He cannot recollect the details, but just barely remembers that someone made a bet that he could drink half a bottle of whisky and then hit a small lamp above the bar with his six-shooter. Needless to say he missed, and then did not want to pay the bet which naturally led to a fight. When Jack woke up, he was in the city jail. The Atchison's sheriff was a pretty tough fellow and for some reason there was no love lost between him and the boys working for Ben Holladay. The moment he found out that Jack was one of Holladay's people, there was no mercy. Under normal circumstances a disturbance like that would be taken care of by a fine and paying the damages, but no jail time. However, this sheriff insisted on a trial and gave Jack no quarter. In addition to his rotten luck, the local judge was out of town and so Jack already spent three weeks in this lousy cell. There could not be a worse punishment for him. Jack, who was accustomed to moving freely around the endless plains and having good food to eat at his disposal, is now in a hole with iron bars that is twelve feet wide and twelve feet long. As to the food the sheriff's deputy brings him twice a day, he doesn't even want to think about it. During the past couple of days he was really becoming desperate. Not that he was a religious person, but occasionally he prayed to God to get him out of there. He promised he would not even look at a whisky bottle. Well, since that did not help, he called upon the devil and kept promising him that he would faithfully serve him until he dies if he can do something about his situation.

In the middle of the fourth week a key rattled in the cell lock. The sheriff's deputy opened the door and a stranger stepped in. Jack happily jumped up to greet him because he was sure that it was the judge which meant the end of his suffering, but the stranger only smiled, pulled an envelope out of a leather case and handed it over to Jack. Jack opened it and there was a letter signed by Ben Holladay announcing that as of today he was appointed the chief of the stage route between Julesburg in Colorado and Salt Lake City in Utah. Holladay needs somebody who would not only be in charge of the entire operation, but who would mainly keep an eye on his employees. Horses and mules keep disappearing, stages are not on time and there is even a suspicion that many alleged attacks on the stagecoaches were actually fraudulent. He received full authority to handle any situation and he can start right away. Jack first thought it was a dream. To be the boss of the entire route is tremendous responsibility, but also the salary was at least three times bigger than he has now. Now he would not have to trudge from one damn place to another because he would have people to do it for him. Jack looked again at the letter, to see if it's not some sort of a joke, but the signature was authentic. Only the looks of that stranger bothered him. He didn't say much and his black piercing eyes kept staring at him. Jack had an unpleasant feeling that he can see all the way to the bottom of his heart. After a while, the stranger interrupted the silence and asked what he was supposed to tell Ben Holladay. "Of course I'll take the job!" blurted out Jack, "but how do I get out of here? They hold me here like a rat." "Everything has been taken care of," answered the man. "The sheriff resisted for a while and wanted a pretty high bail, but when I also offered something for him, he caved in. There is a horse waiting for you in the courtyard. Hurry up." The stranger turned around, stroked his mustache and slowly walked out of the cell. Jack noticed that he was slightly limping on his left foot, and he was about to ask what happened to him, but then he suppressed this thought. Maybe a horse kicked him or perhaps... He did not sleep much during his first night of freedom. He kept asking himself who actually answered his prayers, but then he forgot about it. The fact that he will be the boss in Julesburg made him think about entirely different things.

At the window of a one story stone house sits a pretty young woman. Her black hair reaches her waist and her large dark eyes are bright like stars in the midnight sky. Her firm six foot tall figure suggests that she can handle many a job only men can do. This woman, who is considered the most beautiful female in Virginia City and surroundings, is Virginia Slade. Her lot does not differ from that of the other married women. She is at home alone and spends most of the time waiting for her husband. She is looking at the road from their ranch in Meadow Valley to Virginia City and her face shows worries. Jack has been gone for a week. He was supposed to return with his wagons two days ago, but he had to go through the town, past the saloons which are open the whole day and where whisky flows like water. He had to go through the town where there are many opportunities to get into trouble. Virginia got up, stepped up to the stove and checked the fire. When Jack returns, he will surely want something warm for dinner. Suddenly, she heard pounding of the hooves, the sound she was waiting for so long. Then it occurred to her, why he was not riding his own horse? The short rhythmical staccato belonged to a mustang and not the big full blooded horse Jack owned. She stepped up to the window and below the hill she saw a rider on a small brown horse. A few seconds later the rider reached the house and stopped the horse so fast that it almost sat down. "Missus Slade! Missus Slade!" called the boy. "Go to town right away! There are hundreds of miners there and they want to hang Mister Slade. The miners are everywhere. They sit on the roofs of houses, on the porches and even in the trees and they are armed to teeth. Judge Davis is trying to talk them out of it, but..."

"For Christ's sake, what did he do now?" exclaimed Virginia. "Did he kill someone?"

"No. He just got drunk and got into a fight with the sheriff and threatened some people with his gun."

"Who sent you?"

"Judge Davis."

Virginia had heard enough. She quickly ran and grabbed a saddle and a bridle and then rushed to a small enclosure behind the house where a thorough-bred stallion named Billy Boy was grazing. Billy Boy was originally a race horse which the Blackfeet stole during an attack on a wagon train on the Oregon Trail. He then made it, by some mysterious way, to Fort Laramie where Jack bought him. He bought him for Virginia so she would forgive him for his past misdeeds. Several days before he got drunk and behaved like a mad man and when he got sober, he knew that he would not easily get her forgiveness. Virginia often took Billy Boy to town races and rarely was there a horse that would beat him.

The stallion whinnied and stood motionless while Virginia saddled him up. Once he felt her in the saddle, he trotted out on the dirt road and began to run down into the valley. The boy turned the mustang around and slowly walked back to town.

The crowd was getting louder. Some miners began to recite all the misdeeds Jack had committed during the past months, and some were fairly serious. Judge Davis was getting the strange feeling that he might lose this trial. At least if Virginia were here, then there would be a chance. He looked quickly at Jack, but Jack's blue eyes were staring vacantly ahead into the distance. Jack saw himself stepping out of the stage coach in Julesburg where he was supposed to take over the route stretching all the way to Salt Lake City. He was supposed to replace recently dismissed Jules Beni after whom this route was actually named. Jack knew this guy was a scoundrel but on the other hand he naively believed that showing him the papers signed by Ben Holladay would put an end to his crooked behavior once for all. Well, in this respect he was badly mistaken.

The next day after his arrival, Jack had gone to Jules' private corral and there he noticed that several of the best horses had Holladay's company brand—Jules originally claimed that the Indians had stolen them. The simple task was to lead them back to the company corral and let them join the other horses, but Jules was not going to give up so easily. When Jack was leading the first horse, a large broad-chested brown gelding, a shot rang out and he felt pain in his left hand. He turned around, and then another shot hit him. Jules emptied the whole magazine of his Colt into an unarmed Jack and to make sure that this uninvited guest would never try to cross his plans again, he pulled out of a leather case a shotgun, and for a good measure, fired another shot into the bloodied body. The alarmed and scared station employees dragged the half dead Jack to the stable, placed him on a pile of straw and started to look for a place to bury him. Heaven or maybe Hell itself stood by his side. When after a while Jules came to look at him believing that he would find only a cold corpse, Jack was still alive.

During that night a troop of cavalry came to town. The tired riders surrounded the station and their commander began to look for the station chief. According to the treaty the Holladay Company signed with the army, one of the duties of the stage coach stations was to provide water and fodder for the soldiers' horses. However, Jules Beni was nowhere to be found and it was as if he vanished into thin air. A little bit later, the soldiers found the body of the still-living Jack drilled by bullets. The next morning they loaded him on a stage coach and several days later the military surgeon in St. Louis pulled out of him four bullets and a handful of shots. After such an experience anybody else would have lost their appetite to be the boss of the Julesburg Station, but not Jack Slade. Two months later he was back at work and posted a reward of five hundred dollars to anyone who would bring in Jules Beni dead or alive. Sure enough, one day when a couple of cowboys were looking for stray calves in a nearby canyon, they ran into Jules. There can be no doubt in anybody's mind that they were not going to miss an opportunity to make some extra money. Around midnight they banged on the station gate and, to still sleeping Jack, they handed over their catch for five hundred dollars.

Jack ordered Jules to be tied to a corral post, practically at the same spot where about two months ago he got hit by the first shot from Jules' six-shooter. In the morning he got up early. Thoughts what to do with Jules were racing through his head. Should he hand him over to the sheriff and the court or take care of him by himself? If he hands him to the sheriff, he may escape from the local jail. The judge comes to Julesburg once a month and during this time a bunch of French-Canadians, Rene's compatriots, could break him out. If he metes out the appropriate punishment himself, the word gets around and nobody will even think about messing with him. Jack filled up a glass with whisky and poured it down. Then he took two revolvers off the wall, made sure they were loaded and put a box of ammunition into one pocket and a whisky bottle in the other. He walked downstairs and sauntered to the corral toward the tied up Jules.

The rays of sunshine were slowly burning off the fog and finally emblazed the whole station with a golden glow. Jack had all the other horses taken to another corral and then stood in front of Jules. Again he heard the same voices in his head. Don't! Don't be a swine. You are here to keep an eye on the stage coaches and not to get even. However, the other voice objected. If you let him go, everybody would think you are weak and you know what will happen? They will steal from right under your nose and you'll be a laughing stock. Jack put the bottle to his lips, took another swig and then had a feeling that the warning for decency voice is weakening with every gulp as if it were drowning in a sea of the gold-brown whisky. Suddenly he saw a pair of black piercing eyes. He pulled the gun out of the holster and fired. The eyes disappeared and the bullet smashed into Jules' right shoulder. Jules started to scream and beg for mercy, but Jack no longer heard anything. When he had shot the magazine empty, he reached for the other revolver and kept on firing. Before each shot, he laughed inhumanly and asked Jules where he wanted to be hit. In the belly? Okay, in the belly. In the knee? All right, in the knee. The pool of blood around the victim kept growing while slowly soaking in the dust. Horses scared by so many shots ran wild in the corral, neighed and tried to break out. Finally, the last shot. Blue smoke from the burned gun powder was lazily sinking to the ground when Jack, as if advised by the devil himself, stepped up to still living Jules, pulled out a knife and cut off both his ears. After a while when they untied Jules, the dead body fell in the pool of his own blood.

There is a woman racing on a black horse along the creek, through the valley that leads to Virginia City. The mount and the rider resemble a fairy tale phantom rather than living creatures. Above the stretched body of the horse flies the woman's black hair and the stallion's tail draws a straight line. The horse is in full gallop and dirt mixed with snow flies in all directions. It is the beginning of March, but the northern slopes of the surrounding hills are still snow covered and the creek is in many places locked by ice. Virginia feels the cold air burning her face but there is only one thought on her mind—Will I come in time? As long as they let Judge Davis talk, it will be okay, but when he won't have anything more to say? She passed a little waterfall on her right. From there it was six more miles to town. How many times did I beg Jack to stop drinking!? He could do it for a while, but then... It was as if he was afraid of something and tried to escape from it. As if he tried to find refuge in that damn whisky. He often said that he heard voices or sometimes he mentioned black eyes, but by then he was already on the way to town, to saloons where he drank himself unconscious or into a rage in which he had no idea what he was doing. How about those human ears on his watch chain? He never told her where he got them. If she insisted on knowing, he only laughed and talked about respect. However, this is not a laughing matter. Once the miners got him, they won't let him go. Last year they organized a Citizens Committee to restore order in the whole area and get rid once and for all of all thieves, murderers, cheating gamblers and rogues. My God, if the Nevada City miners got him, they will take care of him like they did the Plummer gang. This committee tries quickly and if they find him guilty, then they know only one kind of sentence—a strong limb and a rope. God, please, make sure that Judge Davis keeps talking! Please give my horse the strength and stamina so that I won't be too late! God, please, stand by me as never before! There were at least three more miles to town. Billy Boy, covered with sweat, shines like polished ebony and his red colored nostrils breathed out clouds of steam. Virginia feels his rapid heartbeat. Then she reached the top of the hill and looked down at the town below.

The yelling was getting stronger and one could hear impatient calls from the crowd. "What's going on? How long will it take? We didn't come here to listen to this crap. Why the hell does he keep talking about Virginia?" Then somebody laughed, "We're not trying to hang her, are we?" but Jack did not hear. The rapid stream of thoughts carried him to Fort Halleck where he was supposed to pick up food supplies and deliver them to Fort Laramie. The army paid well and Jack knew if the wagons arrived on time and no food was spoiled, a fat bonus would follow. So he and his buddies decided to go and celebrate before the trip. After midnight he was barely conscious and when he was staggering toward the barrack reserved for the teamsters, he suddenly saw Jules Beni. He was leaning forward, with blood streaming from his wounds and his eyes glowed like red charcoal. Jack pulled out his Colt and shot the whole magazine into the specter in front of him. The apparition disappeared, but at the same time a loud explosion shook the ground and one of the buildings was ablaze. One of Jack's shots hit a barrel full of gun powder. It was a sheer miracle that he did not get hurt, but the fort commander did not have much sympathy for this kind of behavior. He complained to Ben Holladay and shortly thereafter Jack received a letter of dismissal, just like Rene Jules did a year ago. However Jack was like a cat. He always landed on all four feet and he always survived any trouble. If they don't want me to haul stuff, I'll go and raise cattle. I have a young strong wife, so we'll build a ranch and deliver cattle where it'll be needed. Gold was discovered in Alder Gulch, so we'll try it in Virginia City. Everybody there thinks of gold, but you can't eat it. There is also a good chance that those black eyes won't find me there. Well, for a while it worked. Jack built a ranch and the miners bought everything it produced. They particularly paid for eggs and milk with gold. All he had to do was to hitch up a wagon, take several cows to town and gold was chiming in his pocket. But there were saloons in town and where there are saloons, there is also whisky and so the vicious circle started to close.

Jack's thoughts were slowly returning to the present. Why did they go to that cursed theater yesterday? By that time he and Bill Fairweather were totally stoned. Bill kept saying, "Come on, it's gonna be fun. They got bunch of new broads there. A certain Kate Harpe. Her legs are supposed to be out of this world." So he went, but when Kate appeared on the stage she was only singing and on top of it she was dressed up from her ankles all the way to her neck. Now, that's not what they paid for. Then, as if possessed by a devil, he got up and started to yell at her, "Stop that screeching and show us legs!" The audience was not amused and called the sheriff and here Jack made another mistake. When the sheriff arrived at the theater, Jack pulled out his gun and started to scream that he was Jack Slade who was the boss of the Julesburg route and that no sheriff was born yet who could lock him up. He ripped the warrant out of his hand, tore it apart and ran out. Suddenly in the middle of the dark street he again saw those black eyes. Enraged he fired all six shots, but this time the eyes did not disappear. Mad as hell he grabbed a kerosene lamp hanging on one of the carriages in front of the theater and threw it at them. The eyes vanished, but after a while one could see yellow flames licking the entrance to the local brothel. By now a rider was rushing through the dark night toward Nevada City. By the morning the entire committee had arrived accompanied by several hundred miners. Now he stands on a wooden box under a beam, tied up like a calf before the slaughter. The judge is trying to save him, trying to explain away his behavior, appealing for mercy and understanding, but all he can see are blank stares. If Virginia were here, she would surely save him. She always did. When he was in trouble, she appeared like his guardian angel and saved his skin. Where is she now? Judge Davis stopped talking because he probably does not know what else to say in his defense. Suddenly, a tall man wearing a black coat stepped up close to the box. He is limping on his left foot and he throws a rope over the beam and places a noose around Jack's neck. Now he sees his face. His eyes, his black piercing and glowing eyes—it's the stranger from the Atchison jail. Jack is trying to pray. Tears are running from his blue eyes. His shaking lips prattle something that sounds like Our Father in Heaven, but now... "For god's sake stop! I hear the familiar pounding of hooves. It's her horse. It's Virginia! For god's sake, please..."

Somebody kicked the box away. Jack's body twitched several times and then became motionless. The pounding of hooves is getting closer. The crowd makes way and a black haired woman jumps off her horse covered with cakes of lather and mud. Everybody is silent. Suddenly, this awful deathly silence is interrupted by the piercing shriek of a hawk, or...was it perhaps the triumphant laughter of the devil himself?

Historical Notes

Jack Slade, originally Joseph A. Slade, was born around the year 1823 in Carlisle, Illinois. His father and his brother were both elected to the U.S. Congress, so one can say that his family belonged to the leading citizens of Clinton County. The first official record about Jack Slade is from the period of the war with Mexico. He enlisted as a volunteer and served in the infantry. After the attack on Chapultepec he was promoted to the rank of sergeant and the record indicates that he was decorated for bravery. After the war he went to look for his fortune in the West. In the early 1850s he worked as a teamster and wagon master for the Hockaday and Liggett Company along the Central Overland route. In 1858 he became a stage coach division superintendant and when the Pony Express took over this route, he retained his position. The incident with Jules Beni, a corrupted station master with a criminal past, happened in 1860. A year later in August 1861, Beni was gunned down by Slade. (Some historians believe that it was Slade's people who shot him.) Slade's exploits spawned numerous legends, many of them false. There is another killing which is not disputed and that's the shooting of Andrew Ferrin. It happened in May 1859 when Andrew, who was one of his subordinates, was hindering the progress of a freight train. Slade apparently suffered from schizophrenia, which was getting worse under the influence of alcohol. When sober, he was a pleasant and reliable individual, but when drunk he became dangerous. Ben Holladay owned the route after the Pony Express went bankrupt and dismissed him in November, 1862. The Citizens Committee in Virginia City warned him several times, but under the influence of the public which demanded law and order and because of his continuous rogue behavior they finally decided to execute him. Actually, a rather trivial event decided his fate. After the incident with Kate Harpe, Slade and his crony Fairweather upset a wagon loaded with cans full of milk. It was the last straw that broke the patience of the local inhabitants. There were three dairy cows in the whole area for about three hundred children. People literally paid with gold for a pitcher of milk. The execution, which took place on March 10, 1864, was the last one carried out by the Citizens Committee. As Judge Davis anticipated, the Montana citizens did not agree with the punishment and considered it excessive. Slade could have been, for example, banished from the county or from the entire Montana Territory.

The past as well as the maiden name of **Maria Virginia Slade** is unknown. Historians believe that she married Slade around the year 1857. She was definitely considered the most beautiful woman in Virginia City and the surrounding area. According to a romantic version but not supported by any evidence, Jack and Virginia got acquainted during a game of faro which was followed by a shootout and Virginia, who at that time made her living as a prostitute or a dancer, saved Jack's life. In addition to her beauty she could also ride a horse and shoot like any man. In spite of Jack's shortcomings she was his faithful and dedicated companion who got him out of trouble of his own making more than once. She covered the distance of twelve miles between their home and Virginia City in record time and it is believed should she have arrived in time, she would have stopped the vigilantes from carrying out their sentence. After the execution she rented a house in town, ordered a metal coffin, filled it with alcohol and placed the body inside. She refused to have him buried in Virginia City, but because the stage coach road was still closed, she had to wait till June to have him buried elsewhere. Then with the coffin attached to the stage coach she traveled to Salt Lake City where she intended to bury him. According to one source the coffin was unloaded in Ogden (Utah) at the railroad depot. Since it was not claimed for several months, it was sent to Salt Lake City where it was interred in a pauper's field on July 20, 1864. After she returned to Virginia City, she married Jack's firned James Kiskadden on March 22nd, 1865. The couple moved to Salt Lake City but the marriage did not last long and they divorced March 12th, 1868. The rest of her life is subject to many speculations. Some of her contemporaries claim that she married Elhener Crosby in 1883, while others believe she moved to St. Louis, Missouri. Her death is also surrounded with rumors. She may have died in Omaha, Nebraska or in Chicago, Illinois, however most of these oral versions agree that the once most beautiful woman in Virginia City died owning a house of ill repute.

5

"Soapy" Smith

(Based on True Events)

The game called "Soap" is very simple. All one has to do is to cut a bar of soap into small pieces and in the presence of the players wrap them in small packets while adding into each package a banknote of different value. Then the packets get mixed up in a basket and the players, after having paid a certain amount, can pull out one packet. If they are lucky the banknote wrapped with the piece of soap has higher value than the amount they paid.

Peter Jennings was in a good mood. The trip from Seattle to Skagway took exactly four weeks just as he was told by the clerk of the shipping company who had sold him the ticket. Not only did he arrive on time, but along the way he met a very affable guy who was making this trip for the third time—a certain McConnell, John McConnell. He introduced himself as a representative of a mining company specializing in industrial gold extraction in Alaska. The management of the firm wanted to know all the details about the current situation in areas where gold was discovered. How many people reached Dawson and how were they equipped, how many stores with mining equipment existed in Skagway, with what assortment of goods and what were their prices? They just wanted to know everything before they went into it big and if he may advise him as to the prospecting tools or equipment, he would get the best deal at Brownell & Co. They had a store on the main street at the very end of town. If he was not mistaken, it was the last building on the right and he must definitely tell them that they got recommended by Jack from Seattle. His name is the surest guarantee that they will provide excellent service and above all, they won't rip him off! When the impatient travelers stepped on to the primitive pier, McConnell shook his hand, wished him good luck and disappeared in the commotion of the landing area.

Jennings disembarked with only one suitcase because he liked to travel light. Whatever I'll need, I'll buy in Skagway, he thought and reached into the pocket of his jacket to make sure that his wallet full of fifty and hundred dollar bills was still there. He looked around and decided to take a stroll through the town before paying a visit to the Brownell & Co. After four weeks spent on the rocking deck of the steamer he could not wait to feel again the firm ground under his feet. By the end of the summer 1897 when the gold fever was in full swing, the Skagway population was approaching five thousand people. Most of the town consisted of wooden structures or even tents, but some banks or saloons were already located in solid brick buildings. Jennings crossed the main street full of muddy ruts left by wagons hauling various goods from the landing area and stepped on a wooden sidewalk. He walked into the first saloon he spotted, ordered a glass of cheap whisky, chatted a little bit with the barkeep and then set out to look for the store so he could equip himself for the trip to the Klondike gold fields. He found it without any problem. It really was at the end of town, but it was no longer one of the last buildings, since during the past two months several saloons, stores and livery stables sprang up right next to it. The store owned by the Brownell & Co. was a low one story building covered with weatherboards with the company sign nailed next to the door.

Jennings stepped inside. A small bell at the door chimed loudly, but the man sitting on a wooden box and reading a one month old newspaper did not move, as if he couldn't care less about the new customer. Jennings looked around the room and noticed that it was practically empty. He expected shelves full of shovels, picks, pans, ropes, canned food, simply all the stuff a starting prospector or argonaut would need, but all he could make out in the dark room was a pile of blankets in the corner. He loudly cleared his throat to attract the attention of the man on the box, but he just raised his head, spat the tobacco juice right in front of Jennings' boots and was about to keep on reading. Jennings, however, didn't wait when he disappeared again behind the paper and asked if he could have the honor to talk with the store owner, Mr. Brownell. The man realized that this guy would not let him peacefully continue reading the paper, so he folded it and growled something that sounded like, "Yeah, I'm Brownell." Jennings immediately, heeding polite manners, introduced himself and asked with some hesitation if one could buy here an appropriate mining outfit. Then he added quickly that Mr. McConnell, that is, Jack from Seattle, sent him. However, judging by the empty room, he believed it must be a mistake and that he was about to leave.

The moment Jennings mentioned Jack from Seattle, Brownell's behavior surprisingly changed. He rose quickly, heartily shook his hand and inquired where he met him, how Jack was doing, and then readily added that, of course, they sold mining equipment. As a matter of fact, everything is in the next room, because in here it is just an office where they arrange the whole purchase and then they would look at the desired items. Of course, Jack was right, their prices were reasonable, the goods were of high quality, unlike in other stores where they mostly try to cheat their customers. Now, how much stuff did he want to buy? Jennings scratched his head and then admitted that he actually did not know, so he would leave it up to Mr. Brownell, because he had certainly outfitted many people like him. As an expert, he would know the best what he would need. However, he would be willing to spend around thousand dollars, and then he quickly added, in cash of course. A broad smile covered Brownell's face; he nodded his head and assured Jennings that for this kind of money one could get a pretty good outfit.

Jennings sighed with relief. He would have another fifteen hundred left for Dawson and if he did not waste time here in Skagway, he could buy a good claim directly on the Klondike for a reasonable price. Brownell then excused himself, explaining that he was to take care of something in the warehouse and disappeared into the adjacent room. Jennings heard him talking to another man, and then somebody slammed the door, as if leaving the building. Brownell returned after a while, and again apologized saying he had to give instructions to an employee. "So, let's write it down, shall we?" He pulled out of his pocket a piece of wrinkled paper and a short stump of a pencil. When he was about to open his mouth and ask Jennings something, somebody kicked the door open and a lanky fellow with a black kerchief covering his face and a gun in his right hand stepped inside the room. First he aimed it at Jennings, then on Brownell and ordered, "Keep them up and don't try anything stupid!" Both men silently obeyed. The robber then pressed his gun to Jennings' ribs, reached into his pocket and expertly fished out his bulging wallet. Then he turned toward Brownell and got hold of his money in exactly the same way. "Now, you stay where you are and don't even move! You wouldn't get too far!" He meaningfully waved his gun and slipped out of the door.

The whole robbery did not last more than two minutes. Brownell was the first one who recuperated from the initial shock. He ran out of the store, but the fellow with the black kerchief had vanished into thin air. Brownell started to wave his hands and call, "Help! Help! Armed robbery! Anybody, please help!" He kept running in front of the store for a while, but when nobody responded to his not overly convincing calls for help, he went back inside. Jennings was still standing on the same spot where the robber had helped himself to his money. His knees were shaking and it took some time for him to understand what had happened. All the money, which was supposed to finance his gold seeking adventure, was gone. It occurred to him that maybe it was just a joke the local toughs play on the newcomers. He latched on to his thought and when Brownell returned, he tried to get some sort of explanation. To his amazement, Brownell sat down on the box, opened the newspaper and began to read as if nothing happened. "It was just a joke, right?" Jennings carefully inquired. "Yeah, right a joke. Damn bastards do this all the time, but I got them figured out. I don't carry more than ten bucks, so they don't get rich on my account. If you think that was a joke, go across the street and ask the barkeep in the saloon. You'll see, he'll tell you." Jennings staggered out of the store half conscious, walked into the saloon and headed straight for the bar. There he spouted out the whole story, and wanted to know if someone saw a tall guy with a black kerchief over his face and a gun in his hand. Once he finished, he asked if it was a joke, some sort of hazing directed toward the greenhorns, and then he wondered when and where he'll get his money back. "Well, if it was a joke or not, I don't know, but it happens in Brownell's store quite often. The best thing to do is to talk to the sheriff. He usually hangs around Clancy's Saloon. It's downtown, near the landing area," said one of the customers, who sat near the bar and overheard the whole story.

Jennings walked out of the saloon and ran along the wooden sidewalk back to the center of the town. He burst into Clancy's Saloon covered with sweat and red in the face. "Where is the sheriff?" he shot out all breathless at the bar-keep. The man behind the bar put down a glass he was cleaning and responded with, "And what do you want from him?" Jennings described again the whole event, and added that if it was a joke, it was time to quit. It's getting dark, he will need money for a hotel and tomorrow he has to buy the outfit for his trip to the Klondike. The barkeep just kept nodding his head, then poured him a glass of whisky and with a certain degree of empathy said, "Pour it down because you will need it, even though I'll try to break it to you gently. See, jokes like that don't happen here. The truth is that some scoundrel simply robbed you and

Brownell and because you could not see his face and could not identify him even if he stood in front of you right now, you can kiss that money goodbye. That whisky was on the house and if you want to, I'll pour you another one." Jennings was thunderstruck. So that's what it is. A hoodlum robs you and an honest store keeper and nothing can be done about it? He swilled down another glass of whisky and began to see everything red. "I won't forget about it. I'll complain in the sheriff's office and if it does not help, I'll see the mayor. It is unacceptable and scandalous!" Then he turned toward the other guests and tried to make them join him in his indignation and convince them that something should be done about it, but most of them pretended that they either didn't hear him or that the problems of this tipsy greenhorn were of no interest to them. One guest, who sat alone at the table, carefully followed every word Jennings said. He was a tall older man with a thick black beard, attentive eyes and good natured expression in his face. He wore a long black coat and a soft hat and his long slim fingers, which were definitely not accustomed to work with a pick or shovel, played with a golden watch chain attached to his vest. An outsider would believe that he was a parson or a preacher who wanted to spread the gospel among the argonauts crazed by gold fever. Jennings yelled out that he would make sure that the whole world would find out about the injustice he suffered here and walked out to look up the sheriff's office. The man in the black coat paid and walked out following him. The visit at the sheriff's office turned out exactly the same way as the barkeep predicted. "If you cannot identify the perpetrator, how do you expect me to find him? I cannot make miracles," and with this comment the sheriff led Jennings out of the door. Alcohol, the bitter feeling of injustice and the precarious situation broke Jennings down. He sat on the sidewalk and began to cry like a little boy. Suddenly, the tall man in the black coat stepped up to him, addressed him and asked the reason for his sorrow. He spoke English like that of an educated man with a soft southern accent and when he heard what had happened to Jennings, he sadly nodded his head, and condemned the depravity and moral decay of many people these days. When Jennings admitted that he was cured from his gold fever and he would prefer to return to Seattle, the stranger pulled out a wallet and put two one hundred dollar bills in his hand, saying that he should go home and think of God rather than how to get rich quickly. Jennings barely managed to stutter words of thanks as the unknown benefactor disappeared in the night.

Only when on the ship taking him back to Seattle did Jennings find out that the charitable stranger was the most feared man in Skagway, namely Jeff

Smith, aka "Soapy" Smith. Jennings never realized that Brownell and McConnell were the people who set him up.

A couple of days after the incident in Brownell's store about fifty people secretly met in a warehouse near the landing pier. They were mostly owners of saloons, hotels, outfitting stores and livery stables, in other words, decent citizens, whose primary concern was the wellbeing and prosperity of their town. The meeting was stormy and a casual onlooker would quickly notice that this gathering was divided into two camps. Frank Reid, the local land surveyor, spoke for the smaller group and Billy Saportas for the bigger one. Reid was actually one of the founders of Skagway. He came with the first wave of argonauts and helped divide the flats into building lots. He came straight from Oregon where he had worked as a teacher in the Willamette Valley. Reid was a righteous man about whom no one could say anything bad, and who hated dishonesty and lying. He learned hard lessons in the West and life taught him one thing, namely if the truth is to prevail, somebody has to stand up for it. It's why he had called this meeting to stir up the leading citizens into action against the embodiment of all evil in Skagway—"Soapy" Smith.

"Citizens," he addressed the gathering, "it cannot go like this any longer. Look, Smith holds the whole town in his hand. All his flunkies terrorize decent people, rob the new arrivals and argonauts on their way to the Klondike. A few days ago they robbed someone at Brownell's. They not only operate here, but also in the whole vicinity. It is so bad that nobody would dare to go into the White Pass alone. He's got his spies everywhere and I would not be surprised if one of them is even here today. The sheriff is afraid of him and many people cooperate with him because he has either bribed them or threatened them. A day doesn't go by without hearing about some criminal act caused by him or his gang. People, think of our town's reputation! If word gets out in Seattle or San Francisco that a real arch devil and his thugs rule Skagway, everybody will make a big circle around us and go through the Chilkoot Pass." Noise and yelling voices interrupted Reid. Billy Saportas, editor of the local paper *Alaskan*, who got his job directly through Smith, began to speak.

"Friends, what all of you have now heard is just god damn slander. I can personally vouch for Jeff. Let anybody who got into trouble here raise his hand. See, practically nobody. Jeff is a good administrator. His people make sure that we have order in town. If a bunch of argonauts get drunk, lose their money or blow it in a saloon, you cannot blame Jeff. Do you know how much money he gave to charity and for the construction of a new church? Five thousand dollars! How much did Reid give?" Approving mutter filled the room which Reid quickly interrupted. "Yeah and who knows that about a week later the money disappeared without a trace."

"Women's tales," Saportas cut him off. "No one can prove that Jeff had anything to do with it. How about the support money he pays the widows who lost their husbands? Now, what are you going to say about that?"

"Widows? What widows?" laughed Reid. "Of the fellows whom Smith's thugs have murdered, and you call that charity?" The meeting's participants engaged in a stormy exchange of views and mutual accusations rained from both sides. When the crowd calmed down, Saportas resumed his speech in Smith's defense. "It is all nonsense; lies and made up stories which cannot be proven. I am just interested to hear what Reid will find objectionable about Jeff's opening a draft office and recruiting volunteers to fight the Spaniards? It's a highly commendable show of patriotism and everybody can go Clancy's Saloon and read the Thank You Letter directly from the Secretary of War in Washington, DC. It is hanging there on the wall. So, what are the doubters and all those envious characters going to say now?" The room fell silent. Everybody was really wandering how Reid would explain this. "Well, if you want to hear that, I'll be happy to shed some light on this so called draft office," answered Reid. "Anybody who shows up there and wants to sign up must strip naked in one room and in the other room some clown pretending that he is a doctor examines him. When the draftee in question comes back to get dressed, he finds out that all his valuables like his wallet and watch are gone and if he doesn't like it, they throw him out half naked in the street. It is this, my friends, that Saportas calls patriotism. People, please use your heads!"

Appealing to common sense, however, did not produce the expected results. The majority again condemned Reid and his accusations as irresponsible attacks on a truly honest citizen, who was actually the toast of the town. Suddenly, a short red haired fellow, probably an Irishman, who sat in the corner and listened attentively to the stormy debate, got up and climbed on an empty box of canned food. How he got into the warehouse was not clear because he arrived about a week ago and therefore he certainly did not belong among the so called leading citizens of Skagway. He waved his hands and when he got the appropriate attention, he spoke in a quiet voice, "All right, I'll tell you, who

"Soapy" Smith is. I wasn't sure for a while, but when I saw him at Clancy's Saloon two days ago, and from what I hear now, well, I tell you, there cannot be any mistake. In the early nineties I was working a silver claim in Colorado in a town called Creed. I don't know if you are familiar with this place, but when I got there, "Soapy" Smith behaved as if he owned it. He used the same tricks you have mentioned here a while ago. He did nothing else but played 'Soap,' relieved everybody of his money and if someone dared to resist him, they went pretty soon three feet under the ground. The mayor was Bob Ford, that was the guy who got Jesse James, and Creed served as a hiding place for him from Jesse's brother Frank. Now, Smith had this mayor and the sheriff in his pocket within a week. If the silver ore had not dried up and someone in the end didn't bang off Ford, he would have probably been there still today. So, if I can give you any piece of advice, you'd better get rid of this snake. He is smart like a coyote, but dangerous like a rattler. Personally, I don't care as I am on the way to the Klondike, but if you all don't want to wind up seriously hurt, then..."

"Then what?" cut him off Saportas. "My fellow Skagwayans, you are not really listening to some bum, who keeps throwing dirt on Jeff, are you? What would be the future of our town if we allow any vagabond to interfere with our civic affairs? Throw him out!" Sure enough, several pairs of willing hands reached for the red haired stranger, but he realized that he had overstayed his welcome, jumped down from the box and disappeared into the cold night. Saportas then threw around a few more statements praising Jeff Smith and as expected, most of the present citizens agreed to do nothing, because after all, Smith and his boys support the local businesses, particularly the saloons, and if couple of disgruntled individuals or Bible thumpers don't like it, to hell with them. As for that red haired fellow—good riddance. They had almost started to believe him. Fortunately he won't stay long. The sooner he leaves for the Klondike, the better. We don't need agitators like this in our town.

Well, the trouble was that the red haired stranger never made it to the Klondike. Two dates later they found him not far away from Skagway shot in the head.

About a year passed from the day when the meeting at which the local business people decided not to interfere with "Soapy" Smith's affair, took place. Smith, who had his people at the meeting, was well informed about the opinion of the majority of citizens and because it was positive, he decided to take advantage of it in a really big way. Shamelessly, he conducted his criminal activity without impunity. He even went so far that in spite of the fact that there was not a single telegraph pole in this entire area, he opened a telegraph station from which the uninformed argonauts could send a telegram to their friends or relatives in San Francisco or in Seattle informing them that they reached Skagway in good shape, and if they paid something extra, they could even receive a reply. Food, however, grows the appetite, and as we know, the trees don't grow all the way to the sky and eventually pride will have a fall. Smith's fall came so fast and so suddenly that it was really hard to believe.

It happened sometime at the beginning of July. Around noon one could see two men running along the main street toward the landing area. At the pier, they split. One ran to Reid's log house and the other one burst into the warehouse owned by Captain Sperry. Both men brought the same news and they spread it among the local citizenry as soon as possible. It did not take long for the whole town to know what had happened.

J. D. Stewart was returning from the Klondike. He was one those few argonauts who were lucky and really found gold. In order to bring it safely to the nearest port, he decided to join a group of travelers who headed through the White Pass to Skagway, which was led by Charles de Witt and Calvin Barkdull. Among Stewart's belongings loaded on pack horses and mules was also a large leather poke with gold valued at many thousand dollars. Stewart's friends warned him not to go through Skagway, but Stewart definitely did not feel like spending weeks on the Yukon River on the way to Saint Michael located on the Pacific Coast and then God knows how many more weeks back to British Columbia. After all, what could happen to him? Once in Skagway, he would keep an eye on the poke day and night. Stewart, however, underestimated the prowess of the Smith cronies. Right after his arrival in Skagway two men paid him a visit—Tripp and Bowers. They pretended to be gold dealers, and in an incredible way they succeeded in convinced him not to carry the gold south, but rather sell it here because he would get much more for it than in Seattle or Vancouver. The best deal, of course, he would get at Clancy's Saloon.

At the saloon, a tall man dressed all in black welcomed Stewart, introduced himself as a representative of the Wells, Fargo and Company and invited him to step in the adjacent room where on a large table stood a gold weighing scale. The man in black asked Stewart to hand over the poke, and when Stewart obliged him, he took out of his pocket a magnifying glass, looked at a few grains of the gold dust and began to weigh it. Suddenly, several fellows who looked liked argonauts filled the room. They had heard that somebody had brought gold from Klondike and they wanted to see it. The man in black agreed and the poke circulated among them for a while, until a guy standing near the door slipped it into his pocket, ran out of the room and disappeared among the pedestrians. Stewart realized that there was something terribly wrong and insisted that the man in black do something about. He, however, assured Stewart that it was just a joke and not only would he see into it, but the poke would be returned to him right away. Then he ordered a glass of whisky for him and walked out. That was the last time Stewart saw the alleged representative of the Wells, Fargo and Company. He waited for about an hour, but when he did not show up, he looked up de Witt and Barkdull and complained about the welcome he received in this town.

Around two o'clock a pretty large crowd headed by Captain Sperry gathered in front of Clancy's Saloon. Sperry demanded that the gold be returned immediately and the thieves punished. If the poke was not back in Stewart's hands by four, the newly formed Citizens Committee would take care of it by itself. Smith stood at the bar and while occasionally sipping whisky said something about the rabble needing a lesson. No one would threaten Jefferson Smith, the absolute ruler of Skagway or even give him an ultimatum—him, who got a "Thank You Letter" from the Secretary of War in Washington, DC. Let them come at four o'clock. and he'd be waiting for them.

Shortly after three o'clock the curious crowd began slowly trickling back to the saloon. Finally somebody decided to go after "Soapy" Smith, but he won't give up that easily. It looked like this trouble would end in a row and no one wanted to miss it. During all that time Smith had not left the saloon. He just leaned against the bar and kept consuming one whisky after another. It seemed that vanity and hardheadedness blinded him. Suddenly, he grabbed the Winchester that was hanging on the wall, ran out and began to yell, "I'll show you, you bastards, to make fun of me! You've picked the wrong guy! Go to hell or you'll see!" The scared crowd backed off. "So what are you waiting for?" he bellowed madly and began to shoot, fortunately only in the air. Of course nobody expected anything like that and people dispersed like scared chickens.

Several men turned around and ran to the landing area, to the same warehouse where the citizens meeting took place a year ago. A new meeting was called up and this time it was Sperry who was in charge. He wanted to make sure that before he went to Clancy's to demand the return of the stolen gold he would have the backing of most of the people. The mood was quite different this time than last year. Most of the leading citizens changed their minds not because of some moral principles, but rather they understood that their business interests would be seriously damaged if Smith's criminal activity did not get drastically checked. The gold fever on the Klondike was over. Thousands of argonauts possessing large amounts of gold would be coming back, and the shortest way from Dawson to civilization was through Skagway. If these people find out what happened to Stewart, they would avoid the town by a large circle. They did not suffer all that hardship, frozen and sometimes going hungry, to be robbed by some crook. Of course they could care less that the Skagway businesses would come up short. If the city fathers could not keep law and order, all that money they would have to spend along the way for food and lodging would be spent somewhere else in more decent places. The argument met a positive response. During a stormy discussion it became obvious that most of the participants no longer intended to keep closing their eyes when Smith's roguery was involved and decided to stand on the side of the law.

Meanwhile, Smith had returned to the saloon with a triumphant smile on his face. "What did I tell you? Bunch of cowards, that's what they are. One only has to fire a couple of shots and they fill their pants. Now, I'll go to the pier and give them the same treatment." He reloaded his Winchester and put in one pocket a Colt .45 and in the other a small Derringer. Clancy, the saloon owner and a long-time Smith friend, warned him, "Come on, don't be stupid! Those guys in the warehouse are armed. Those people here were just curious onlookers, but down there you will run into Reid and Sperry. Sperry is an old soldier and he won't run after the first shot." "That remains to be seen," scornfully sneered Smith as he stepped out. Skagway turned into a ghost town. After the shooting in front of Clancy's Saloon practically everybody realized that things were getting serious and, of course, nobody wanted to take chances that he may get hit by a bullet fired either by Smith's gang or a member of the Citizen's Committee. If they really start shooting, lead would fly from all directions. As to Smith's gang, people did not have to worry. Most of his cronies were already gone or on the way out of town. Smith at this moment had no idea that he stood against the whole town entirely alone.

When he showed up at the pier, the meeting was in full swing. The cold wind blowing from the ocean carried excited voices from the warehouse where this time the gathered citizens demanded radical action against "Soapy" Smith. Smith however, confidently grinned, turned off the safety on his rifle and stepped forward. At that moment somebody blocked his way. "That's far enough!" he heard Reid's voice call out. Reid was patrolling in front of the warehouse to make sure that none of Smith's people could sneak in and interrupt the meeting. "I believe that your game is over. If you value your life, you'd better return that gold and get the hell out of this town! As a matter of fact, many people brought enough rope to this meeting to have a hanging party." Smith thought that the moment of surprise would be on his side, but instead of it he ran into Reid. "I'll take care of you in no time," he growled and raised the rifle. Reid quickly grabbed the barrel, pushed it aside and pulled out a gun. Smith exclaimed, "Don't shoot," but Reid had already pulled the trigger. Instead of a deafening shot, one could only hear a sharp click. The gun misfired. Smith reacted quickly. Somehow he managed to aim at Reid and fired. Reid fell with a shattered hip, but at the same time he squeezed the trigger again. This time his revolver did not fail him and as another shot rang out, Smith collapsed, hit in the chest.

Hearing gun fire, the citizens ran out of the warehouse. A dying Smith was rattling around on the ground and next to him Reid lay in pain. Trying to smile he uttered a few broken sentences, "It's okay boys. I got him. He won't do any harm now. I just got a kind of strange feeling in my left leg. It's as if it is all on fire."

The citizens carried Reid to his log house, where he later died. The dead body of "Soapy" Smith lay on the spot where the bullet from Reid's Colt hit him for several days. When the judge searched Soapy's apartment to prepare a list of his belongings, he opened his trunk and there on the bottom among other things lay Stewart's poke of gold.

Historical Notes

Jefferson Randolph Smith, otherwise known as "Soapy" Smith was born in Georgia and he used to pass himself off as the son of rich plantation owner. As a young man he attended school to become a Baptist preacher, but did not finish his studies. He married soon after leaving school and upon his departure for Texas, he left behind a wife and six children. He had one brother who joined the editing board of *The Washington Star* newspaper in Washington, DC. Smith worked as a cowboy for a while and then took part in a cattle drive from Texas to Colorado. He never came back to Texas and we can also say that this was the last time he made a living by honest work. In Leadville, Colorado, he met a certain man named Taylor, who invented the game of chance known as "Soap." Smith mastered this game in a very short time and he played it so well that he quickly earned the nickname "Soapy" Smith. In 1892 he arrived in Creed, Colorado, and his stay in this mining town became a sort of preparatory or testing phase for his later "rule" of Skagway. After the silver deposits in Creed were exhausted, he moved to Denver and in 1887 he and five of his trusted cronies surfaced in Skagway. Let's have a look at these individuals, who with Smith formed the kernel of the Skagway underworld. **Charles Bowers**, who had the nickname "Reverend Father," was a dangerous criminal and a killer, who often played the role of a priest or a preacher. **Syd Dixon** was a con man, gambler and a drug addict. He came from a rich family and by his manners and the way he dressed, he made the impression that he was more a playboy than a criminal. **George Wilder** was a con man with great acting talent. He usually pretended that he was a businessman or representative of a large company. (In the story he is portrayed as John McConnell.) Thanks to his ability to convince people that he was an upstanding citizen, he gained the confidence of many rich people and information about their finances. For Smith's fraudulent "jobs" he played the essential role of a spy. Another important pair were **Slim Jim Foster** and **Red Gibbs**, who usually carried out the dirty and violent jobs. It is also important to mention an interesting fact that Smith, after his arrival in Alaska, checked out two other cities, **Wrangell** and **Juneau**, to settle in. However, the city administration, and particularly the law enforcement in these two towns, was fully consolidated and smoothly working, so Smith picked the third town, namely Skagway, where due to general chaos the conditions for his criminal plans were much more conducive.

A whole slew of historians asked the question later on: How was it possible that most people did not see his true nature? The answer is relatively simple. Smith was able to fully and perfectly cover it. He could assume the role of a priest, plantation owner or a businessman and always make an impression that the only thing he had on his mind was the wellbeing of his fellow man. Quite often he stood on the right side of the law, e.g. when the excited mob wanted to lynch Ed O'Keefe for murdering Bob Ford, Creed's mayor, he faced the crowd and insisted on proper legal proceedings. When in Skagway, he supported the striking longshoremen and in doing so he secured their respect and admiration. He regularly gave money to charity and various religious projects. Another important factor in his successful, though criminal, career was being thoroughly informed. At the peak of his nefarious activities he had in his service about two hundred people, which included newspapermen, bar owners, barbers, prostitutes and pimps. Practically every important official was in some way or somehow indebted to him. In addition to an army of spies who provided information about what was going on in town he exchanged letters with a number of politicians in Washington, DC, such as Senators, Congressmen and lawyers. All in all we can say that Smith's "regime" was in a way a predecessor of modern dictatorships. On the surface it was philanthropic, but inside it was criminal and he stayed in power by condemnable means.

After the shootout at the pier, the whole gang intended to disperse, but its members soon found out to their surprise that there was no way to escape from Skagway. On one side there was the sea and on the other the White Pass protected by the Canadian Mounted Police. The Citizens Committee caught and arrested up to thirty gang members within 24 hours. Bowers, Tripp and Foster were detained a few days later. The excited mob wanted to take care of this trio immediately and on the spot, but only the timely arrival of the militia from the neighboring town of Dyea (lying at the foot of the Chilkoot Pass) prevented the lynching. Later on they were all transported to Sitka, where they were tried. The sentences varied from one to ten years. Saportas and the other fellow travelers managed to buy tickets for the steamer Tartar which was leaving for Seattle. In this way the cleansing of Skagway was completed. In conclusion, we can say that neither the Baptist nor Methodist parsons wanted to bury Smith. In the end it was the Presbyterian Church official, J. A. Sinclair, who carried this task off under the protection of several members of the Citizens Committee. Smith was buried in the same cemetery where a few days later Reid was put to rest. While Smith's grave is marked only by a simple stone with a name, Frank Reid has a small monument with the following inscription: "He gave his life for the honor of Skagway."

6

Major Wolcott Marches on Buffalo

(Based on True Events)

t was the hot summer of 1886. The sun mercilessly burned the last remnants of grass on the vast pastures stretching from Cheyenne to the Montana border. The old timers watched with worries as the herds of cattle lost weight and would not be ready for the long winter. This year's winter came early and with it an unusual amount of snow. In some spots the snow reached four feet. At the beginning of March the southwesterly warm wind, the Chinook, finally started to blow which usually melted the snow away so cattle could graze again. However, this year it did not blow long enough and there was still a thick layer of snow on the ground.

Suddenly, the temperature dropped and instead of warm weather a blizzard arrived. The thermometer dropped below zero, the old snow turned into a sheet of ice and the fresh snow formed a new layer two or three feet thick. The cattle were definitely cut off from the grass. Cows and newly born calves wandered in the snowstorm or gathered near the empty barns of the individual ranches as if looking for help, but people in their snow covered dwellings plugged their ears so they wouldn't hear their desperate mooing and curse God for their misfortune. Several weeks later, the cattle turned into walking skeletons, then collapsed in the snow drifts and froze to death. Another foot of snow covered their carcasses. Only horses survived. Icicles several inches long hung around their muzzles, but they didn't give up and persistently broke the ice with their hooves to get to last year's grass.

When the snow finally melted away, the endless Wyoming pastures were covered with tens of thousands of dead cows, steers, bulls and calves. Small as well as large ranches reported losses between sixty and eighty percent. Some were completely ruined and those which survived had to face incredible difficulties. At that time a new evil surfaced. The evil, which spread among the local ranches was caused by the people themselves—cattle rustling spread like wild fire. The herds of cattle which survived the 1886–1887 winter did not grow, but were getting smaller. The cattle were disappearing like snow in the spring sun. As the ranchers could not eradicate this evil in a legal way, they decided to take the law into their own hands.

Jack Cooper was a cowboy who worked not far from the Searight's ranch. His favorite trick was to change the H brand into 0-0. When he was charged by the cattle association in Cheyenne, the judge, because of a lack of evidence, let him go. However, a year later Cooper was shot and killed by an unknown hired assassin.

Elle Watson, aka Cattle Kate, was known for buying stolen cattle and instead of money she offered whisky or sex in return. Her partner, Jim Averell, then rebranded the cattle and sold it in the neighboring states. One day, in the summer of 1889, six masked men arrived at their ranch, handcuffed the suspicious couple, hauled them to the nearest canyon and hanged them.

Tom Waggoner was supposed to be a friend of the big ranchers. Nevertheless, in the fall of 1891, three men passing themselves off as a sheriff and his deputies, detained him and took him away. Eight days later the neighboring ranchers found him hung on a tree in an isolated canyon.

"Ranger" Jones was shot in ambush by a hired killer or killers fifteen miles from Buffalo. His neighbor found him dead, sitting on the driver's box of his wagon loaded with lumber for his new stable.

John Tisdale was shot in ambush by an unknown assassin not far from Buffalo during Christmas 1891. His dead body lay on top of the Christmas gifts he had loaded into his wagon that were meant for his family.

In all cases the victims were suspected of cattle rustling.

In March 1892, Cheyenne was not only the capital of Wyoming, with which, as to the size, only Denver in Colorado could compete, but it was also one of the fastest growing cities east of the Rocky Mountains. It was the richest city in the southern part of Wyoming and the center of the cattle region along the

Sweetwater River. The richest, because an average ranch owned several thousand head of cattle and tens of thousands of acres of grazing land. Cheyenne was also connected with the rest of the world by a railroad, which not only supported the business, but also promotes social and cultural life. An opera theater was built in 1882 and in 1884 the famous Lily Langtry, aka Jersey Lily, performed there in the play *Pygmalion*. The attention of the local citizens, however, was not focused on the opera theater, but rather on the Cheyenne Club, a two-story Victorian stone building decorated with carved ornaments.

There, on the wooden terrace, stood the known local ranchers who were involved in a lively debate, all gesturing energetically with their hands. There was still snow on the ground as other owners or foremen of big ranches kept arriving in their luxurious carriages. Here came Hubert Teschemacher, a young elegant Bostonian, and Frederic O. de Billier, a New York aristocrat, who decided to invest in the cattle business with close to a half million dollars. Next was William Irvine, a foreman of a big ranch owned by several millionaires from Omaha and shortly after him arrived Fred Hesse, an Englishman, who allegedly worked his way up from a common cowboy to the director of a cattle company which owned vast acreage of the best pasture land in southern Wyoming. And, of course, Major Frank Wolcott, one of the most active members of the association was also present. He was from Kentucky and came to Wyoming in 1869. He had received several thousand acres from the federal government and now owned one of the largest ranches near Glennrock.

Curious onlookers admired the pure bred horses, fancy carriages and expensive harnesses, and from time to time they wondered what must be going on that all these "cattle barons" have suddenly gotten together. They may be considering a new law or regulation that pertains to the cattle business. When these modern "lords" cook up something, even the governor thought twice about opposing them, and any of their decisions are good as law whether someone likes it or not. No, Sir, one cannot joke with these gentlemen.

The terrace emptied out around noon. The ranchers strolled into the club dining room, where they were served salmon, sea eel, artichokes, lobster and other fine cuisine which the guests washed down with champagne or other fine French wine. After lunch everybody walked to the conference room where, while drinking coffee and smoking expensive cigars, they decided to tackle the problems at hand. Major Wolcott opened the meeting. He looked at the present members of the cattle association, cleared his throat and started, "Gentlemen, allow me to address right away the most important point of our agenda, namely the ever growing cases of cattle stealing. As you know, the arrogance with which the newcomers obtain land and start their beggar ranches is unprecedented. Not only do they disturb the integrity of large grazing areas, but moreover their herds grow with fascinating speed, while ours are rapidly getting smaller. All attempts by our cattle inspectors and range detectives are frustrated or directly sabotaged by the courts and sheriffs, who just simply look the other way or, even in some cases, they enter into the trading of stolen cattle themselves. The case with Cooper fully supports this argument."

Calls expressing agreement interrupted Wolcott's speech and when he added that Cooper deserved his punishment, all forty one ranchers broke into a loud applause. "Gentlemen," Wolcott continued, "patience has its limits. We tried for several years to rectify the situation through legal and administrative actions. We prepared a black list which was supposed to get rid of all thieves and parasites in our state. We decided to put some order into the cattle branding and registry of individual brands. How did the rabble near Buffalo and their leader Sheriff Angus react? They founded their own cattle association and decided to ignore all the current regulations dealing with branding and sale of the livestock."

Again, exclamations of disgust and indignation interrupted Wolcott who proudly looked around. It seems he had gotten everybody's support, so maybe it was time to strike while the iron was hot. "Gentlemen, you will certainly agree with me, if I tell you my opinion. To keep treating these lowlifes with kid gloves is utterly useless. Therefore, I think it is time to apply a radical solution. Before we talk about this item, I must ask you to make sure that we are alone because the stuff I am going to suggest must stay absolutely secret." Two or three men obligingly stood up and walked out in the corridor to see if it was empty and then one of them volunteered to stay in front of the door, just in case some unauthorized person got inside and try to eavesdrop.

"Gentlemen, I propose to conduct an expedition to Buffalo and liquidate all criminal elements in one clean sweep." Only a bomb exploding in the middle of the room would have caused a bigger shock. First, a grave like silence fell, but gradually one voice after another spoke in favor of Wolcott's proposal. Why not? We tried to be good guys for many years and what did we get? Sneered and laughed at. They ignore the laws and call us barons and plutocrats. If a man did not keep an eye on them day and night, they would steal all his cattle right under his nose, but this would teach them a lesson. We are lucky that Major Wolcott is one of us. He is an old soldier and during the Civil War he fought in the Union Army. His military experience would guarantee total success.

When the ranchers calmed down, Wolcott continued, "I took the liberty to put together a list of all undesirable individuals whom the justice system should have taken care of a long time ago." Major Wolcott pulled out a folded sheet of paper from his pocket which contained almost seventy names of small ranchers and cowboys from the northern part of Wyoming who were to be liquidated or driven out of the state. On the top of the list was the Buffalo sheriff, W. E. "Red" Angus, who was known for his leadership of the local ranchers and his consistent refusal to investigate any complaints about cattle rustling presented by the ranchers from the south, and three other members of the local government residing in Buffalo. The next one was Nathan Champion, who was driven out of Colorado for stealing cattle, and right behind him followed Nicholas Ray, a known cattle rustler and a dangerous gun slinger. There was even a bounty on his head because he killed two men in Texas. Further down on the list there was John Flagg, who edited the Buffalo newspaper and kept systematically attacking the ranchers in the southern part of Wyoming. The rest was made up of the names of newcomers who settled near the big ranches and so were automatically considered suspicious.

The sheet of paper circulated among the ranchers and each of them marked one or more names of people whom they believed it was time to get rid of. When the list returned to Wolcott's hands there was not a single name which was not checked at least once. Wolcott folded the sheet, carefully put it back into his pocket and resumed his speech, "Friends, allow me to make you acquainted with some details of this operation. As a former army officer I strongly believe that fifty men could do this job. I have obtained already nineteen volunteers from our ranks, and in addition to these nineteen brave men I also have the honor to mention that Frank Canton is willing to go with us." As soon as the gathered men heard the name of Frank Canton, they all responded by nodding their heads and muttering approval, because Frank Canton, the former sheriff from Buffalo, had become the association's detective and apart from being an excellent shot he also demonstrated effective organizational skills. "One of our detectives," Wolcott continued, "Tom Smith, a former Texas lawman, is willing to go back to Texas and hire the rest of the gunmen, which would be mostly his friends. If there are no objections, I would like to mention the cost. A daily salary of five dollars plus food and ammunition, fifty dollars bonus for each rustler killed and three thousand dollars for life insurance. Naturally, we will take care of the transportation, horses and the other necessary equipment."

Wolcott's final announcement was followed by a lively debate. Some, without giving it much thought, were ready to realize his plan, but others were more careful, and warned about the consequences of this action. It was undoubtedly against the law. If it were leaked that they agreed on it ahead of time, then it was premeditated murder and one could hang for it. Maybe one should find a way to avoid direct responsibility for such a drastic measure.

Suddenly, the door flew open and the rancher who was patrolling outside, stepped in. He was all red in the face and in his hands he held the Buffalo newspaper which had arrived this morning. A banner headline announced that the northern ranchers would start the annual round-up one month earlier than called for by Wyoming law. In other words, the pastures would be full of thieves rounding up unbranded cattle belonging to the big ranchers while they sat at home and waited for the legal date. Well, that was that. That's not a provocation; it was a declaration of war. When the excited ranchers calmed down and Wolcott asked them to vote on his plan, all forty-one hands shot up as if following a military command.

Early in the afternoon on April 6 a strange train pulled into the Cheyenne depot. It had passengers and one mail car, three freight cars full of horses, and finally one flat bed loaded with brand new red painted wagons with a pile of camping gear such as tents, collapsible beds and cooking kettles. Right after its arrival it was moved to a separate rail where it stayed till evening. A couple of curious onlookers kept ogling it, but who the unknown passenger was they could not establish because the curtains at the windows were tightly pulled together. During the course of the evening thirty passengers boarded this mysterious train, which then left the station late at night and headed toward Casper.

Who were those people who patiently sat the whole afternoon inside the passenger car and who were those individuals who under the cover of darkness joined them? Tom Smith fulfilled the job Major Wolcott assigned him to the letter. He succeeded in hiring twenty-five men, mostly former sheriffs or deputy sheriffs who were now willing to enforce the law of the territory of Wyoming and protect the interests of the big ranchers. They were all armed to the teeth. Each man had a Winchester and at his belt either a Colt or a Smith &Wesson revolver. They were not all the same age, but one thing they did have in common is that they were all hot blooded Texans. They all met in Denver the previous night, where a special train was waiting for them and now they sat in one part of the Pullman and played cards. The other section of this car was occupied by a mixed group of folks.

First and foremost were Major Wolcott and his nineteen volunteers. Those men were mostly foremen from the ranches located along the Sweetwater River, such as Bill Irvine and Fred Hesse, but also a number of men from the ranches along the Powder River. Namely, Frank Laberteaux from the ranch owned by Henry Blair, Louis Parker from the Murphy's cattle company and Charles Ford from the TA Ranch. In addition to the ranchers and foremen this group also contained six range detectives and cattle inspectors, who, apart from their mastery of a six-shooter, had a thorough knowledge of the terrain and essential information about those seventy people slated for extermination.

An interesting character was Harry Wallace, an Englishman and rancher from Colorado, who joined the expedition for rather romantic reasons; simply, he wanted to experience an adventure and when he heard about the Wolcott's plan, he signed up. The other two men seemed to be out of place, but no, it was not a mistake. They were journalists. One was the editor of *The Cheyenne Sun* and the other of *The Chicago Herald*. When they promised that they would describe the whole event from the point of view of the big ranchers, Wolcott agreed to take them along. The last person clearly indicated that Wolcott was a soldier in body and soul. As an officer he knew that the fighting might get bloody and that's why he had engaged Dr. Charles Penrose from Philadelphia. Penrose was visiting in Cheyenne and when he heard about the march on Buffalo, he joined the gunfighters, motivated mainly by curiosity rather than longing for an adventure.

Both groups, the ranchers and the Texans, kept to themselves. The Texans didn't show any signs of worry and most of the time they played cards, joked and from time to time had a swig of whisky they had brought with them in good supply. As to the plan of action and the strategy, that was not their business. Let those worry who hired them. They were here to shoot and they knew that damn well.

On the other side of the Pullman, however, there was a serious debate going on. Wolcott, who was by all other men acknowledged as an expedition leader, was explaining his plan, "Gentlemen, about this time the telegraph line between Buffalo and the other railroad stations should be cut off. We will load all our stuff on the wagons in Casper, mount and head north. The first night we'll spend at the TA Ranch and the next day we'll reach Buffalo. The moment we liquidate Sheriff Angus as well as the town and county officials, their glorious association will be without leadership. Then we'll hit the individual ranches and all that scum will disperse like a herd of sheep. Considering the fact that we have fifty men who know how to handle weapons, it should be a piece of cake. I figure it shouldn't take longer than three or four days."

Shortly after midnight the train stopped at a small railroad station. Wolcott and Canton stepped out and pretended they wanted to send a telegram to Buffalo. The man in the telegraph office, however, informed them that it would not be possible since the connection had been interrupted for several hours. Wolcott and Canton politely thanked him and with a contented grin on their faces got back on the train. Wolcott's people in Buffalo obviously carried out his orders.

The train reached Casper about three o'clock in the morning. Under Wolcott's supervision the men first started to unload the horses, then the wagons and finally the camping gear. After a while the Texans agreed among themselves who would ride which horse, and as soon as they hitched the wagons, the small army moved out to Buffalo which was a distance of about one hundred fifty miles. The trip, however, didn't go exactly as Wolcott imagined. There was still snow at the foot of the Big Horn Mountains, the dirt roads were very muddy and the small streams, which they had to ford, were pretty high. The wagons sank up to their axles in mud, the horsemen had to help the draft horses and at one spot, to make the situation really maddening, the bridge collapsed under the weight of a team. Cursing galore, it took more than an hour to free the wagon and the horses. By afternoon it was clear that they would not spend the night at the TA Ranch. Then suddenly the sky got dark and before anybody could understand what was going on, a snowstorm struck. The march had to be stopped, horses unhitched and tents put up and because they had traveled mostly through a flat and open landscape, there was not a tree as far as they could see to tie up their horses. They had to use underbrush, or some, who had enough foresight, brought wooden sticks which they drove into the ground. I guess the reader can well imagine how the Texans felt.

In the morning, after having spent a sleepless night, they staggered out of the tents and to their great horror discovered that half of the horses were gone. The snowstorm had subsided a bit, but it still took them about half a day to round up the horses, pack up the tents and get ready to continue the trip. Needless to mention that Major Wolcott was mad as hell. Around noon a rider could be seen in the distance. Judging by the way he rode, there was no question that he was in a hurry. He did not spare his horse and headed directly toward Wolcott's cavalcade. When he was about a quarter mile distant, Ford from the TA Ranch recognized him as one of his cowboys. In another minute or two the man on a lathered horse arrived and out of breath rapidly told them the news, "There are rustlers at the KC Ranch!"

Well, nobody planned on that happening. They were supposed to keep on going to Buffalo, but Wolcott and the other ranchers seemed to prefer a sparrow in the hand over a pigeon on the roof. The idea that after that horrible night and troubles along the road they would finally have an opportunity to take it out on somebody, prevented them from thinking rationally. The only one who kept a clear head was Canton. He was fully aware that a handful of thieves would endanger the much greater plan, but nobody listened to him. The ranchers and Wolcott had their minds made up. How about the Texans? Well, they couldn't wait until their repeaters and six-shooter would finally get a chance to speak. That's the reason they came here, wasn't it?

So after a short vote, the majority decided to take care of the rustlers first. But Nature, as if it wanted to show them the silliness of their decision, turned against them. The blizzard came back in full strength and the self-appointed protectors of law and order spent almost the whole night on the road before they covered a miserable fifteen miles. Twice they had to stop and make fire to prevent frostbite. Only before sunrise did they spot the buildings of the KC Ranch.

The KC Ranch consisted of two buildings—a log house and a barn. Originally it belonged to the Frewen Cattle Company, but after its break up it was purchased by certain man named Nolan. Now it was basically abandoned, but because it was located at an intersection of the main road to Buffalo and several side roads, the local ranchers used it as a shelter during time of inclement weather. As not a living soul had visited this place for weeks on end it was also an ideal hideout for rustlers. While it was still dark the major placed his men in the barn, close to the nearby creek and in the brush behind the log house. The group was so tight that even a mouse wouldn't make it through.

At the crack of dawn the log house began to show signs of life. First, one could hear voices and after a while the door opened and two men stepped out. The men lying behind the log house turned off the safety on their rifles and looked at Canton. He shook his head. Those two were trappers who hid there from the blizzard. Judging by the pots they were holding in their hands, they were going to the creek to get water. Canton was right. Both bearded fellows walked down a mild slope directly to the creek. The moment they submerged the pots in water, they heard the sound of several pistols being cocked and then a quiet voice ordering them to put the pots down and step closer to the bushes. If they made a sound, they would never have an opportunity to fetch water again. Both trappers obeyed and slowly walked to the underbrush.

Once they got out of the viewing angle of the log house, two Texans stepped out, tied them up and brought them to the barn where Wolcott was waiting. A short interrogation revealed that Canton was right. The Major then ordered both trappers held in the barn and only released when they were done with the siege. After a while the door opened again and this time Nick Ray stepped out holding a bucket in his hand. He looked around, probably wondering what had kept the trappers so long, and then he decided to go to the creek by himself. At that moment, however, Wolcott nodded his head and a young Texan, who had the nickname The Texas Kid, pulled the trigger of his repeater and hit Ray squarely in the chest. Ray staggered back, then a salvo of shots hit him and he collapsed just a few steps from the log house.

Right at that moment the door opened again and in the door frame stood Nate Champion firing his six-shooter with his right hand and with his left hand pulling Nick inside. The door closed again and the KC Ranch fell silent. One could hear only the faint chiming of empty shells falling on the scattered stones as Wolcott's men were reloading their weapons. Five or ten minutes later Wolcott sneaked out of the barn and called up a war council. According to the trappers, there were are only two men in the log house. One was now dead or on his last leg. Champion was armed with plenty of ammunition, so he could keep us here for quite a while. To shoot at the log walls would not make any sense. Any ideas? At that moment, just out of the blue, a light wagon, sort of a flat bed, which the ranchers used to haul wood, appeared on the road. It had come from the Big Horn mountains toward KC Ranch. Two horses pulled it and the driver sitting on the wagon box was a boy, perhaps sixteen years old. Wolcott readily gave an order, "Hit the ground, so he doesn't see us!" The boy arrived at the intersection and because the ranch did not show any signs of life, he turned left and kept going toward Buffalo.

Inside the log house, Nate Champion pulled out from his pocket an old notebook and pencil and started to write notes. He mentioned both trappers who went to fetch water and never came back and then Nick Ray who was dying. When he was just about to write about the boy and the wagon, he noticed that on the same road that the boy had come on, a horseman appeared and was now headed straight for the ranch. The stranger had no idea what was going on there and only when he got closer did he spot several men standing at the enclosure behind the barn. He seemed to know them, or at least some of them. It was Major Wolcott. He would recognize him in any crowd because he was short and stocky with his head leaning to the side, a result of a fight with a cowboy at Fort Laramie. And the other guy? It was Bill Irvine. However Bill Irvine immediately recognized the man on the horse. "That's Jack Flagg! We have to get him!" and he and several other men were already running to their horses.

Yes, this stranger was Jack Flagg who, whenever he could, attacked the big ranchers and their association with the newspapers. Now he was on the way to Gillette where he wanted to catch a train to Cheyenne. The Wyoming Democrats held a sort of a convention in Cheyenne and Jack, as the representative of the North Wyoming Democrats, didn't want to miss it. The sixteen year old boy, who was driving the team about a quarter mile ahead of him, was his stepson Alonso Taylor. He was on the way to Buffalo to get boards and beams to build a new barn. Jack realized that the situation was quite serious.

He turned his horse around and buried his spurs into its flanks. The horse neighed and took off in full gallop behind the wagon which was about this time in the middle of the hill. As soon as the boy heard the thundering of the hooves, he turned his head. He saw Jack waving his hands and yelling to whip the horses and drive like hell. Once they got behind the hill, it would be okay. There were a couple of trees up there where he could get covered and cool them off with his Winchester. Alonso cracked the whip and the horses took off. The top of the hill was rapidly getting closer, but then the shots rang out down at the creek. Some bullets broke the spokes and several bullets hummed by the boy's head. The horses were covered with sweat and the traces were taut like wires. A few more yards and they would be safe. The boy, in order not to fall, pressed his legs against the footrest and his left hand clutched the reins so tight one could see the white of his knuckles. His right hand held the whip.

Suddenly, the near-side horse, a small bay, fell. The wagon skidded several times and then came to rest. Alonso jumped off the box, followed by a dismounting Jack, who helped him to unhitch the other horse, a large grey gelding. "Jump on him and ride as if a thousand devils were chasing you!" exclaimed Jack. "We'll meet at Smith's ranch. Tell everybody what happened! This is not something personal because with Wolcott and so many other people here it will be something big!" Alonso didn't wait any longer, jumped on the horse and drummed with his heels on the grey's ribs. A few more jumps and he cleared the crest of the hill. It now looked like he'd get out of this without a scratch, but how about Jack? How would he get out of here? He quickly looked back and saw Jack standing behind a tree, aiming his repeater into the valley with his finger on the trigger.

Nate carefully looked out of the window, first toward the creek and then at the hill where a while ago he saw an unknown rider and a boy with his team. On the road he spotted a group of riders led by Bill Irwin as they were coming back to the ranch. They were coming alone. Nate had a warm, satisfying feeling. They did not get them, not even their horses, which meant that if he could hold up at least till the evening, help might not only be on the way, but would also arrive in time. He was sure that those two guys would rouse most of the ranchers between the Powder River and Buffalo.

Well, the trouble was that Major Wolcott was aware of this too. They had to get serious now. They had to get that guy in the log house at any cost and as soon as possible, otherwise the moment of surprise would be gone. Somehow at the bottom of his heart he admitted that Canton was right when he insisted they keep going on to Buffalo, but there was no time to waste on remorse. Wolcott ordered firing at the log house from all sides. Nate, however, fought back like a devil. If somebody tried to get closer, his Winchester or Colt drove them back. When they tried the other side, he covered the open space with lead as well. If the shooting subsided, he opened the notebook and scribbled a few words. Judging by the sun, one could tell that it was late afternoon, and...no help. Nate began to get an uncomfortable feeling that he might not be able to get out of this mess. Well, if he wasn't going to be able to tell about it to anybody, at least a few of his lines would.

The Major finally realized that just shooting at the log house was not the way to get Champion. They could spend another day here. He looked desperately around as if he were seeking some idea how to finish this fiasco when his eyes caught a glimpse of the upset wagon on the hill. He thought for a moment and then slapped his forehead and silently called himself a super idiot. How come it did not occur to him earlier? A few minutes later a group of men rode off to fetch the wagon. They cut off the dead horse, hitched one of their draft horses and drove it to the barn. There they loaded the wagon with old hay and couple of boards they ripped from the barn.

When Nate looked out the window to find out what was going on, he saw four men pushing the wagon to the front door of the log house. At the same time several shots drove him back inside. One of the men then carefully leaned out and threw a burning match on the wagon. It did not take long and the wagon turned into a burning torch and a while later the fire spread to the log house. Nate understood that the game was over. He quickly wrote goodbye to his friends, signed the last sentence with his full name, Nathan D. Champion, and firing both weapons—his revolver and Winchester—he broke out the back door believing he would be able to reach the nearby underbrush. It took only four shots to prevent him from ever telling his friends how he had held Major Wolcott and his fifty men pinned down at the KC Ranch for the whole day.

Alonzo was leaving the place where he saw Jack for the last time in a sharp trot. He did not want to push the grey too much because he knew that he would need all the stamina he could muster, and also the anxiety of what happened to Jack sort of kept him back. When he suddenly heard the thundering of hooves, he pushed the horse into a canter fearing that the men from the KC Ranch were on his heels, but then he pulled him back again. He heard Jack's familiar voice, "It's okay. They didn't dare to follow me over the open terrain, but now we'll split. I'll go left and warn the ranches at the foot of the Big Horn and you go right in the direction of Crazy Woman Creek. We'll meet then at Smith's ranch." Alonzo nodded, turned the horse to the right and crossed a snow drift. The wet snow balled up on the horse's feet, but there was no time to clean them. He rode into a hollow and after a while he disappeared from Jack's sight.

The sun hid behind the clouds and a sharp wind began to blow. Alonso felt it penetrated all the way to his bones. Moreover, he lost his gloves during this row. He probably left them at the wagon when they were unhitching the grey. From here to the Smith's ranch it was a good thirty miles. If he didn't get frost bitten, it would be a miracle. About an hour later he crossed a small creek. It could be Crazy Woman Creek, he thought, but it definitely flows into it. If there is any ranch in this area, it will be near water anyway. He was right. About five miles further he spotted a small unfinished house with a thatch roof. Probably a newcomer. He could hardly finish his thoughts when a man appeared on the porch and aimed his rifle at him. Alonso immediately began to swing his hands and yell, "Don't shoot!" Then he spouted out everything that happened to him and his stepfather Jack, and that they had lost a horse and that Jack was warning the other ranchers between Big Horn and the road to Buffalo. The man lowered his rifle and asked, where he was supposed to go. "Everybody is meeting at Smith's ranch," answered Alonso, and then inquired if there were any other ranches on the way to Smith Ranch. "Yes," the man said, "there is one along Crazy Woman Creek."

Alonso reached Crazy Woman Creek at dusk. Here he made a mistake that almost cost him his life. He saw a light in the distance and being convinced that it must be the rancher's house, he kicked the horse into a canter and headed straight for the main entrance. Almost simultaneously he saw a flash followed by the crack of a rifle. Those days nobody would allow a stranger to come just like that, directly to the house, particularly at night. It was Alonso's great luck that he missed. The boy started to scream that he was Alonso Taylor from the ranch on the Red Fork owned by Jack Flagg and that he was bringing important news. The rancher listened attentively to the whole story and dryly remarked that it was good that it had already started. "Now we'll clip the aristocrats' wings once and for all. Then he ran into house and returned with a saddle and bridle. "Go inside. Let your horse rest and have some coffee. It's about eight miles from here to Smith's ranch. I'll ride ahead, and if I see Jack, I'll tell him you made it okay." Alonso gladly accepted the offer and slipped off his horse. He took a few steps and slightly moaned in pain. Since he rode without a saddle, his tailbone was rubbed raw and his thighs burned because of his rolled up pants. First he watered the grey and then he entered the house. He carefully sat down on a chair and the rancher's wife placed a metal cup of hot coffee in front of him.

Later, it took him about two hours to cover the distance of eight miles to Smith's ranch. At the hitching post and along the fence stood several dozen horses and inside the main building he could hear the excited voices of men. Alonso slowly dragged himself to the door and stepped inside. He looked with his tired eyes over the whole crowd and then sighed with relief. Jack was standing in the corner talking to the owner of the J. R. Smith ranch. Alonso's heart was flooded with a good feeling that in the end everything turned out all right. They both escaped without being harmed, and moreover they managed to warn a pretty good number of ranchers and these guys will know how to handle Wolcott.

About an hour later, he fell asleep in the adjacent bedroom buried in blankets. However, he did not sleep for long. Shortly after midnight the thumping of many feet woke him up. He crawled out of bed, peeked into the noisy room and it occurred to him that something important was under way. The gathered men had decided to act. Some were already outside saddling up while others were leaving with rifles and cartridge belts over their shoulders. Well, whatever they were planning to do, he could not miss it. He got dressed, slipped out of the house and a few minutes later he was leading the grey out of the stable. He tightened the cinch on the borrowed saddle and was about to mount when Jack stepped up to him. "Where do you think you are going? Get the hell back in the house! We are going to stop Wolcott and you could get hurt there. How would I explain it then to your mother?"

Alonso, not knowing what to say, shifted from one foot to another and tried to come up with some excuse when Smith walked by. Having heard Jack's stern voice he felt sympathy for the boy and decided to come to his rescue. "Let him come along, Jack. He is big enough to see how people fight for a just cause. We'll need someone to hold the horses anyway." Alonso threw him a grateful look and waited for what Jack would say. He muttered something that it's okay, but he'd better make sure that nothing happens to him. Alonso put one foot in the stirrup and slowly dropped his sore behind in the saddle. A group of about thirty riders trotted out of the ranch and when they reached Crazy Woman Creek, they urged their horses into a canter.

The moon in the cloudless sky covered the night landscape with a light glow. The snow on the hills glistened with a bluish hue and the alders along the creek threw long shadows. Nobody talked. The horses were breathing heavily and blowing clouds of steam from their nostrils. The pounding of the hooves complemented the chiming of the spurs and rhythmic creaking of the saddles. Occasionally the horses' shoes hit a stone and one could catch a glimpse of sparks. Men and horses resembled more fairytale specters than night riders. After about an hour of riding they hit a broad road. Here three riders turned to the right. Their job was to get to Buffalo as soon as possible and inform Sheriff Angus about Wolcott's commandos and their intentions. The rest of the riders turned to the left toward the KC Ranch. Smith's plan was simple. They would wait for Wolcott and his gunmen here on the road to Buffalo and if they came tonight, they would ambush them.

Major Wolcott stepped up to Champion's dead body, looked around and declared, rather frustrated, that if he had fifty men like Champion, he would conquer the whole of northern Wyoming. Then he ordered the body to be dragged to the nearest tree and Irwin attached to the bloody shirt a sign announcing that this was the way any rustler would meet his end. "All right, we're done here. Mount! Wagons and the other equipment will stay here and we'll pick it up on the way back. We've lost lots of time, so we have to make it up." Major barked a few more orders and about half an hour later the whole cavalcade began moving again. According to his plan they should arrive at the TA Ranch before morning, take a short rest and then attack Buffalo. Wolcott allowed a short break around midnight. The men loosened the cinches and checked the saddle blankets, while some of them made small fires to boil coffee and to warm up a little bit. Then the order came again to mount and ride out. Practically all the men rode in a loose formation, which did not make the major, as a soldier, too happy, but what can you do with undisciplined civilians? However, when it came to the tactical rules, he would not give an inch, and he knew why.

A vanguard consisting of two men rode about a mile ahead of the whole unit. About two o'clock in the morning, both men rushed back and reported that they had spotted suspicious activity in front of them. The Major ordered everyone to stop, dismounted and with Irwin took off on foot to conduct a true military reconnaissance. Those two guys were right. In the darkness one could detect a faint sound of snorting horses. Otherwise everything was quiet. "Probably mustangs," remarked Irwin. Wolcott was about to nod in agreement, but then suddenly, right in front of them, a rifle shot rang out. "Yeah, mustangs," grinned Wolcott. "I'd bet you those bastards found out about us and think that we'll walk into their trap, but they don't know the old Major." Both men returned and informed the rest of the group about the new situation. After a short council Wolcott ordered them to cut the barbed wire stretched along the road and create a large circle to bypass the armed ranchers who were blocking the access to Buffalo.

After a while, to their great surprise, they heard the pounding of hooves caused by Wolcott's men, and then J. R. Smith loudly cursing that jackass and all his ancestors, who fired that panicky shot that gave them all away.

Wolcott and his men arrived at the TA Ranch before sunrise. The escape maneuver was perfect, almost as if it was taken from the military manual for marching tactics. They covered the rest of the way without any trouble and as to the ranchers, they must have vanished into thin air. Now they were only dead tired, cold and without sleep. In view of the fact that they were now on friendly territory, Wolcott allowed a two hour rest. The riders, as well as horses, badly needed it. If they wanted to attack during the day at Buffalo, they'd better get in good shape. Around eight the temporary camp woke up. Men were cleaning horses, checking the tack for any damage and from all sides one could hear opening and closing of rifle breeches and cartridge chambers. Now things would get tough and a broken saddle strap or jammed rifle could cost one his life. Major Wolcott finally swung into the saddle and ordered to mount. Then he raised his hand and was just about exclaim in an old military fashion "On to Buffalo!" when a rider appeared on the road leading toward the ranch. The horse was all lathered and in full gallop, an indication that the rider was in real hurry. All men, including the Major, felt a little bit nervous. A messenger from Buffalo, who rides as if someone's life was at stake, was not a good omen.

Then Canton recognized him. It was Jim Craig, a member of the Cheyenne cattle association. After a few seconds the man jumped off his horse and, breathless, rattled out the news Wolcott was subconsciously most afraid of: the moment of surprise was gone. The whole town was up in arms and a small army led by Sheriff Angus was moving against them. They would be here in no time. Now what? Wolcott called up again a war council and the views differed.

Detectives Frank Canton and Tom Smith insisted on the original plan, while the Texans kept their cool and just stated that they were hired to shoot, so what's the problem? Wolcott and the ranchers, however, did not want to act precipitously and realistically weighed the whole situation. Buffalo had over a thousand people and if they counted the local ranchers, Angus could have assembled two or three hundred armed men. In such a case, fifty gunmen would not have a chance. No, they could not risk a running fight. The ranchers looked at the Major and asked a simple question: what then did he suggest? Major Wolcott did not panic and again proved that he was an experienced soldier. He looked around, judged the terrain and quickly realized that not everything was lost. The TA Ranch can be defended. We'll fortify it and then they would have it out with Angus and his volunteers right here.

Wolcott was now in his element. His spirit traveled back thirty years. He returned to the time of the Civil War when choking smoke and bloodied bodies of soldiers in blue and grey uniforms covered the battlefields of Pennsylvania, Maryland and Virginia. If he had had a battery of heavy guns at his disposal, his euphoria would be complete. Instead, he would have to manage somehow only with light weapons and a bunch of civilians who have no idea how a military operation is carried out.

He ran up and down the ranch the whole day up, supervising the construction of the fortification and in his free time he drilled the Texans as well the ranchers. From a strategic point of view, the TA Ranch was situated extremely well. It consisted of several log buildings. It was built on a sort of peninsula formed by Crazy Woman Creek and on top of it was surrounded by a fence constructed of lodge pole pines seven feet tall. However, the Major was not satisfied with only its advantageous situation. He ordered the men to dig trenches between the individual buildings and out of a pile of logs intended for the construction of another barn, he decided to build a small fort on an elevated spot next to the stable. How, in the evening, did the members of the Cheyenne Club, who were accustomed to lifting glasses of expensive wine and not ten inch beams, feel, anybody can imagine. After sunset they all devoured a pile of boiled potatoes and with a feeling of anxiety about what the next day would bring, they lay down on their primitive beds. Only the guards placed in the haylofts and along the fence were up. They tried to pierce the darkness with their eyes and ears to catch any sign of activity in the vicinity of the ranch, but the silence was interrupted only by occasional snorting of a horse in the corrals and the hooting of an owl.

At the crack of dawn came the moment of truth. The TA Ranch was completely encircled and in all directions one could see smaller or bigger groups of ranchers and volunteers from Buffalo digging trenches and piling up dirt to build firing positions. They numbered about three hundred men. The sheriff, "Red" Angus, returned to town to oversee the supply of ammunition and new volunteers and during his absence a certain "Arapaho" Brown took over the command. Brown was a wild character who did not have much of a sense of humor. He lived several years among the Indians and that was why the moniker Arapaho. His attack plan was not too complicated—to shoot their way to the buildings and then set them on fire. In this way Wolcott and his cattle barons would get the fitting reward for Nate Champion's death. The lead from several hundred rifles began to chew off the wooden walls and splinter the boards and window frames. Since there were among these men several owners of Sharps buffalo rifles, the weather boards of some of these buildings started to turn into kindling. Suddenly, as if fearing that the ranchers from Southern Wyoming and the Texas gunmen could get away, Arapaho ordered his men to open fire on the horses in the corral. The cracking of rifle fire was now punctuated by heart-breaking screams of wounded horses. It was too much for the Texans. A couple of them ran to the crews hiding in the little log fort and in the haylofts, told them to hold their fire and then at a given command shoot in the same direction to cover several brave men who would try, in the rain of bullets, to chase the horses from the corral into the stable.

Toward evening the firing stopped. The major walked around the ranch, visited the fighters in the fort and the other buildings and could not believe his eyes. Except for a few minor scratches, nobody was seriously injured. Considering the amount of bullets fired at the ranch, it seemed to him like a small miracle. Then he again posted guards, particularly along the fence, because he was afraid Angus might try to breach it a night. The mood among the ranchers was not too great. Most of them did not expect these kind of complications. After all, even Wolcott was surprised that the local ranchers were capable of putting up such a united resistance. It was supposed to be a simple job. Basically they wanted to cleanse Wyoming of several criminal elements, but these guys here saw it completely differently. Instead, as if to show some appreciation for his action, they swarmed up like stirred up bees. Who would now prevent them from giving him and his fellow ranchers the same treatment they were preparing for them? These gloomy thoughts were on their minds as they tried to fall asleep, but most of them kept restlessly rolling in their beds the whole night.

The Major got up early. He visited all the crews and then, in military style, asked the night guards to present a report about the enemy's night activity. The guards reported that the enemy camp was basically quiet and the only thing they could see were camp fires. Wolcott remarked that it was good and then muttered just to himself that they should be here by now and that they were obviously taking it easy. The people standing next to him probably wondered who should be here and who was taking it easy, but because the sun appeared over the horizon and the besieging ranchers started their shooting, nobody asked any further questions. The men resumed their positions and returned the fire.

Wolcott went back to the stable and climbed up to the hayloft from where he had an unhindered view of the enemy positions. First he looked along the defense line which was formed by Crazy Woman Creek, but except for the flashes of rifle shots he did not see anything that attracted his attention. Then he walked on the other side and looked in the northern direction and what he saw took his breath away. A large barrier built from logs and bales of hay and placed on two wagons was slowly moving across the open space. The Major could not help himself and uttered a pretty profane curse. The color of the wheels indicated that this entire monster was moving on the wagons they had left at the KC Ranch.

An uninformed reader may ask, So what? All wagons are the same. Well the trouble was that these wagons were full of ammunition including dynamite sticks. If Angus' people attacked with dynamite to break the seven foot high fence, it will be done in a matter of minutes. Wolcott ran down and ordered concentrated fire at the barrier, but the bullets harmlessly disappeared in the hay bales and the mobile fortification was getting ominously closer and closer. Suddenly, a small brown object flew out from behind the barrier. It flew over the open space and landed couple of feet from the fence. In the deathly silence one could hear only the hissing sound of a burning fuse and then an explosion. A cloud of smoke and dirt obstructed the view for a moment, but when it disappeared, the fence was still standing even though it leaned a little inward. In front of it, however, was a pretty deep hole. The defenders cheered, but the barrier began to move again. The next stick would land at the fence or right behind it for sure and it would shatter the fence into pieces.

The red wheels stopped. A grave-like silence fell over the battlefield. Everybody inside the ranch waited with horror wondering when the next stick would fly. Suddenly, out of the blue, they could hear the blaring sound of a military trumpet. On the northern side right at the creek appeared colorful guidons and behind them three troops of U.S. Cavalry. The Cheyenne aristocrats and the Texas gunmen could not believe their eyes. Providence kept a protective hand over them after all. They were saved.

Well, it was not so much Providence as Major Wolcott's foresight that saved them all from an ignominious end. To put it in a nutshell, the Major was as sly as an old fox and as an experienced soldier he knew that he would not be able to hold the TA Ranch against such an overwhelming force for long. The first night he secretly sent a messenger south to inform the members of the cattle association of their precarious situation. It was just like twenty six years ago when Portugee Phillips rushed south to send a telegram to inform Fort Laramie about the Fetterman Massacre. This time another rider galloped through the night to send the telegram from the nearest station. The only difference was that this telegram was supposed to prevent a massacre. However, it was not that easy. Wolcott quite correctly surmised that the telegraph lines would be repaired, but the problem was that the local ranchers came to the conclusion that it would be to their benefit if the connection with the outside world stayed interrupted. The messenger had to ride the whole night and the next day, almost one hundred miles, before he found a station that was not cut off. The telegram actually made it all the way to Cheyenne and the ranchers gave it to Wyoming governor Dr. Amos Barber. He then contacted President Benjamin Harrison and, being a friend of the cattle association, he tactfully omitted Wolcott's participation. He just mentioned that there was civil unrest near Buffalo and requested the assistance of the Sixth Cavalry, which was stationed at Fort McKinney. The president agreed and the very same night under the command of Colonel Van Horn two hundred and forty cavalrymen departed for the TA Ranch, where as we now know, they proverbially arrived at five minutes to twelve.

Historical Notes

The final act of this episode, that is, Major Wolcott's surrender to Colonel J. J. Van Horn, concluded the so called **Johnson County War** in Wyoming. Sheriff Angus vehemently refused to give up Wolcott and his people. He insisted that they should be handed over to his jurisdiction and agreed to their removal to **Fort McKinney** only when Van Horn promised that they would be tried in Buffalo. However, they did not stay there too long and shortly thereafter they were secretly whisked to **Fort Russell** near Cheyenne, which significantly improved their situation. Here they could move freely and to the local population which generally supported their effort to combat cattle rustling they became a sort of an attraction. Several weeks later Buffalo formally charged them, namely with the murder of Nate Champion and Nick Ray, but their defense lawyer, Van Devanter, succeeded in convincing the judge that it would be impossible to form an unbiased jury in Buffalo and therefore guarantee a fair trial. At the same time Buffalo received a bill for daily maintenance of the prisoners in the amount of one hundred dollars per man. Within several weeks the Johnson County treasury was empty and on August 7th the prisoners were set free with the proviso that they would submit themselves to the upcoming legal actions in Cheyenne. The trial never actually materialized because Buffalo could not afford to pay further legal costs and therefore withdrew the indictment.

As a curiosity, one can also add that only one person out of the whole expedition died of injury. Ironically, it was self-inflicted. The Texan **James Dudley** fell from his horse, his gun discharged and the bullet went through his knee. The wound got inflamed and eventually caused his death. Only three other Texans were lightly wounded.

Let's see what happened to the other central characters. **Dr. Penrose** did not take part in the fight at the KC Ranch because he got sick along the way and decided to return to Cheyenne. While stopping at the town of **Douglas** (about fifty miles east of Casper), he was detained, and when later on the news got out that he belonged to Wolcott's group, he was almost lynched. It was only the governor of Wyoming, his friend and also a physician, Dr. Barber, who extracted him from this precarious situation. He issued a warrant for him and ordered his transfer to Cheyenne. There, under the cover of darkness, they put him on the "cowcatcher" of a locomotive with the recommendation not to leave it until it was in neighboring Nebraska. Dr. Penrose later became a prominent physician in Philadelphia and he did not visit Wyoming again until twenty years later.

Frank Canton left for the Klondike during the Gold Rush in Alaska where he held a position as a judge. As an old man he returned to Texas where he died.

The Texas Kid, who fired the first shot at Nick Ray, returned to Texas, but his "law enforcement" career ended quickly. He quarreled with his fiancé, who refused to marry him because of his participation in Wolcott's campaign. During one of those arguments he shot her. Consequently he was tried, found guilty and hanged.

Tom Smith, who hired the Texas gunmen, returned to Texas and also held a position as a judge, but was killed during a shootout with a desperado.

Alonzo Taylor moved from the ranch on the Red Fork to Buffalo where he and his step-father Jack Flagg published a newspaper. Later on he purchased this newspaper and became its sole owner; however, the publishing business was not fully to his liking, so he sold the paper and worked in the oil fields. He died in 1922 at the age of 48 after an accident at a saw mill.

Arapaho Brown was shot by two cowboys at his ranch, but the motive was never fully established.

Major Wolcott and a few other members of the cattle association left Wyoming and managed their ranches through their foremen for many years, but eventually they all returned.

The grey remained until his death at the ranch on the Red Fork.

Nate Champion and Nick Ray are buried in the Buffalo Cemetery.

7
Han-Chi

A full moon illuminated the landscape. It brightly flooded the south-eastern side of a tall mesa and with the help of westerly breeze, broad tops of miniature pines and cornstalks on the little fields on its plateau set in motion a strange play of shadows and light. As the moon continued its journey in the sky, a yellowish red rock wall gradually emerged from the black darkness of the canyon. A light haze suggested that somewhere at its foot flowed a river or a creek.

Suddenly, a large cave appeared in the moonlight, and right in the middle of it, tiny and as if covered with silver dust, stone buildings. The dwellings out of uncut stone stood close next to each other, occasionally interspersed by a tall square tower or a low round structure. Simply put, it was a small town built in a huge cave. At first glance it seemed that all its inhabitants were already sleeping. Nothing disturbed the night's peace, nothing threatened the safety of its dwellers. The rope ladders were pulled up a long time ago so nobody could get into the cave from the canyon and the secret passage from the plateau was known only to those who are now asleep.

However, there was still light in one of the windows of these tiny houses. Somebody was still awake. It was the old Chook-Chi. She kept the fire going and impatiently waited for her granddaughter. From time to time she looked out the window at the rising moon and muttered something to herself. She could not understand what that girl got out of sitting on the rocky ledges at night. She said she was watching the stars, but at night when the canyon was full of spirits every decent person made sure he was at home in order not to provoke them. The only one who knew how to handle them was Kiwo-to, the medicine man and even he did not go out at night if he didn't have to. Crazy kid. When will she finally grow up?

About the same time while Chook-chi was leaning over the fire and prattling something with her toothless mouth, a young about fifteen year old girl dressed only in a short skirt out of rabbit skins sat on the ledge directly above the cave. Her long black hair flowed all the way to her waist and her large round eyes carefully watched the cloudless sky which before the moon rose, was full of stars. Of all the night scenery, they attracted her most. Each was different. Some were big and bright, the others were small, only flickered and they seemed to be far, far away. Once she asked Chook-chi, what are these stars, but she didn't know. Then she asked the medicine man Kiwo-to and he told her that they were human souls. When a human being dies, his or her soul turns into a little flame that rises all the way to the sky and there it shines. Depending on what kind of person he or she was the flame is either big or small. The souls of good people give lots of light and the souls of bad people can be hardly seen. Once she noticed that there were much fewer big bright stars than those flickering, but being fifteen she did not pay much attention to it.

Suddenly, she shivered. The cold air from the canyon reached the ledges and the short skirt did not provide much protection against the night cold. The girl got up, gave the starry sky another look, and ran home. She passed the corn field and pushed aside the thick underbrush at the edge of the mesa. There in the green carpet of the wild blueberries was a narrow trail. It led to a large boulder seemingly blocking the trail. However, between the boulder and the rock wall there was a narrow, maybe a foot wide crevice. The girl slipped through it like a cat and after a while she disappeared behind the edge of the cave. There she ran down several stone steps and in no time stood before the dwelling where she lived with Chook-chi. She lifted a yucca curtain and entered. The fire was still burning and throwing long shadows on the walls of a small room. Chook-chi was sitting on a small flat rock repairing moccasins. The moment she saw the girl, she began to rebuke her that she was not supposed to tempt the spirits and hang outside at night, but the girl only smiled, slipped under her skin blanket, and closed her eyes, still imagining the sky full of stars. Then, almost asleep, it occurred to her. How will her star look when her soul turns into a flame?

The town began to awaken before the sun reached the cave. In one kiva one could hear the mumbling of the medicine man Kiwo-to as he was driving away the night spirits with an incantation. This was one of his morning duties, because until he finished this ritual, no one dared to leave the cave. Now he ceremoniously leaned over a fire and threw into the yellow flames three dried up lizards. The fire cracked, the lizard meat began to burn and choking smoke rose up. The medicine man started to cough, waved his hands as if he wanted to chase the remaining spirits away or perhaps to break up the smoke, and then being satisfied with this exercise, he walked out of the kiva. Watched closely by all inhabitants of the town, he stepped up to the edge of the cave, stretched his hands over the precipice and uttered the last magic formula. If any spirits were still around, this was their last chance to disappear. Shortly thereafter several men unwound the long rope ladders and dropped them into the canyon. A new day in the cave town officially began.

Chook-chi was also up and was crushing corn seeds on a small flat stone. Her granddaughter watched her for a while and then she grabbed two clay jars, put them into two baskets connected with a wide leather strap, threw them over her shoulder and like a squirrel climbed down along the rope ladder into the canyon. When she came to the creek, she saw that somebody was here before her. The water was muddy, as if wild pigs rolled in it. Can't they be more careful, she thought, having in mind the men who came down to the creek with large pots out of burned clay? The town dwellers were building another granary and every drop of water they needed for the mortar they had to carry out from the bottom of the canyon. Never mind, upstream there was a large pool and its water was clear like a mountain spring. She jumped over several small boulders, ran past a rock wall covered with moss and a big dead pine, and there the creek widened and right near the bank there was a pit several feet deep full of crystal clear water. The girl carefully removed the jar from the basket, filled it with water and put it back. While she was filling the other jar, she had a feeling that she was not there alone. She looked around the canyon, but except for several rabbits and a big hawk in the dark blue sky she did not see anything. Spirits could not be here. First, it was already daylight, and Kiwo-to had chased them away. Even if there was one here, she would not recognize it because she had never seen one anyway. She shook her head, put the other jar in the basket and she was just about to hang it over her shoulder, when she suddenly saw a stranger in the brush next to the rock wall.

Her first reaction was to throw everything away and run. The man was not moving and so the curiosity of a fifteen year old girl won over the animal instinct which warned her against anything unknown. She remained and attentively watched the stranger. He was tall, very tall, taller than her by two heads at least. His hair was tied up on the back of his head with a leather strap that held an eagle feather in place. He wore a skirt from tanned deer skin and there was a big stone axe attached to his belt. His feet were protected by moccasins, but unlike hers made out of yucca, his from leather. Now he smiled and raised his hand with the palm toward her. It was the Indian greeting indicating that he came in peace. The girl also smiled and repeated the greeting in the same way. They both watched each other for a while and then the man carefully stepped closer to her. The inside voice insisted that she run, while there was time, but the fact that she saw a man from a different tribe for the first time made her stay.

The stranger finally spoke, but she did not understand a single word. Fortunately Chook-chi taught her the basic sign language which enabled all tribes in that area to communicate.

"I don't understand you," she replied with a hand gesture.

The stranger repeated the same sentence, but this time he accompanied it by a gesture meaning, "Who are you?"

"Han-chi. Who are you?"

"Sawa-Tu-Han-Tala."

"What does it mean?"

"The Son of Big Bear."

"What do you do here?"

The stranger proudly straightened up and answered, "I am a warrior and a scout."

"What does it mean?"

Here the sign language failed. Han-chi never found out the meaning of these words. They were both silent for a couple of minutes and then the girl reached out and touched the strange thing the man had hanging on his shoulder. "What is it?"

"That's a bow," he answered and when he saw in her face that she did not understand, he removed this strange object that looked like a bent rod with both ends connected by a leather thong from his shoulder. Then he pulled out from a leather pouch a long narrow stick with a sharp point, placed it on the leather thong, pulled it, aimed at the nearest tree and let go. The hissing sound of the flying arrow scarred the girl so much that natural instinct finally won over her curiosity. She grabbed both baskets with the jars and ran. In a couple of minutes she was in the safety of the cave town. Fortunately Chook-chi was chatting with the other women and so she never realized that it took Han-chi unusually long to bring water from the canyon.

Han-chi could not stop thinking about the strange man most of the day. At one point she even tried to draw him in the sand inside the cave. She was so busy with it that she did not notice Chook-chi standing behind her watching her effort. Suddenly, Chook-chi asked, "What are you doing?"

"I am drawing a giant," answered Han-chi innocently.

"What do you mean—a giant?" Chook-chi asked quite upset. "Don't you know that only Kiwo-to can draw in the sand? You could call up some bad spirits and bring yourself and the others trouble." Han-chi quickly obliterated the drawing with her foot. She got scared. Chook-chi may be right. What possessed her to draw in the sand? Nevertheless, the image of the stranger kept returning. Something about him attracted her. He was tall, much taller than she and the way he walked, yes, he did not walk like men of her tribe. They walk bent forward and rock. They got it from picking the corn and blueberries and from working in the fields. He walked erect, proudly, as if he were not even afraid of spirits. Only his eyes she didn't like because they were narrow and wandering. As for that awful thing on his shoulder, she'd better watch out for him.

The rest of the day was uneventful. The men kept bringing water and rocks from the canyon to finish the granary, women worked in the corn fields on the plateau and children played among the stone buildings in the cave. Toward the evening Han-chi suddenly heard noise and voices of numerous men. When she walked out of the house, she saw everybody running to the big kiva where the tribe elders and Kiwo-to held council. She could not get in, but from the excited voices coming from inside she figured out what had happened. The men carrying water found in the mud a foot print belonging to somebody from a different tribe. It was an imprint of a moccasin, but not made from yucca, like they wore, but from leather. Moreover the imprint was quite large. The town people were Michi-Maki—Small People. The foot print was left by someone very big, and the old timers know what it meant. Michi-Maki made a living by collecting forest fruits and raising corn, and sometimes they caught a rabbit, or a fox. They were not hunters or warriors. Most of the Big People made a living by hunting big game and when they killed it all, they moved and looked for new hunting grounds and woe to anybody who was in their way. The situation was serious. The old Kiwo-to remembered how they were fleeing once from the Big People and it had taken them several winters before they found this cave. Most of the young people were born in this cave town and many moons had passed before they finished it. If the Big People find us, that will be our end, Kiwo-to lamented.

That night nobody in the cave town slept. No one dared to make a fire, because the smoke could betray them, and people only whispered, so no one could hear them. Then, in the morning, Kiwo-to threw an extra five lizards on the fire to chase away not only the spirits, but also the strange intruder.

But the canyon was quiet. The screeching of a hawk or an eagle occasionally interrupted the murmuring of the creek, but otherwise nothing indicated that there could be somebody there with unfriendly intentions. The town inhabitants abstained from any activity for a few more days, fearing that they could be discovered. They did not even go to the plateau to check on the corn. Eventually a handful of the bravest ventured into the canyon. They returned around noon with calming news. They did not spot anything suspicious, no sign of the Big People or anyone else. Maybe it was a false alarm, maybe it was not even a human footprint. Han-chi during all that time did not even dare to say a word about the man she met at the pool. She felt remorse that she even talked to him and at the bottom of her heart she felt guilty that she did not say anything to their headman. However, the idea of the panic she would have caused prevented her from doing so. So she tried to convince herself that by now he was gone anyway, because either he left by himself or there was a great probability that the night spirits drove him out of the canyon. After all, the men who searched the canyon reported that there was nobody there. However, somehow she was not too sure about it.

In the meantime the Son of Big Bear was hiding in a small cave near the entrance to the canyon. He was slowly chewing the corn seeds with pemmican and kept reproaching himself for making a mistake, for betraying his presence to that young girl. What was he thinking? By now she has told everybody and roused up the whole tribe. Michi-Maki are cowards. They crawl into their rock holes, they will stuff their bellies with corn and they will stay away from the canyon. In this way he'll never find the way into the cave town.

She was really pretty. Maybe he could kidnap her and bring her to his people as a squaw. However, what if they all laughed at him? The tribe was going hungry, so he volunteered that he would find the cave town with granaries full of corn, but if instead of it he brought a little squaw, that would be another mouth to feed. Suddenly, it occurred to him that if he asked her to become his wife she would show him the way into the cave. One thing was sure, if he did not find the way to get into the cave town he would be the laughing stock of his whole tribe. Yeah, really a great scout.

The Son of Big Bear spent several more days meditating over this dilemma and finally decided to go back into the canyon. He walked the whole night, mostly in the creek bed, in order not to leave any footprints. He stepped out of the creek not far away from the pool where he had met Han-chi. He trod very carefully on the rocks and made sure that his moccasins did not leave any imprints anywhere. On an elevated spot he saw a cluster of young pines that would offer not only a safe hideout, but an unhindered view of the rock wall where he believed the cave town must be. He did not waste any time, made sure that no one saw him, and quietly crawled under the thick pine branches. He riveted his eyes on the rock wall and waited. His patience eventually paid off. By sunrise, as if out of nowhere, the rope ladders appeared on the wall and a while later he made out Michi-Maki with large pots climbing down into the canyon. It was a good sign. Either his presence was not betrayed or the cave dwellers had calmed down when they found out that there was no immediate threat. Now all he has to do was wait for when Han-chi showed up.

Han-chi came on the second day toward the evening. Chook-chi found out that all drinking water was gone, and so Han-chi readily grabbed the jars and a few minutes later stood at the creek. The situation was the same as before. The water was all muddy because the work on the granaries was resumed and everybody was rushing because it was necessary to catch up what was missed during the past days. The clear water was, of course, in the pool. Han-chi probably would go there anyway, just out of curiosity. She slowly shuffled along the bank and looked in all directions, but the canyon did not show any signs of life. From the distance she heard only voices of men carrying water and stones to the ladders and then climbing up to the cave. She filled both jars, placed them into the basket, put the strap on her shoulder and...she almost shouted in surprise. Near the rock wall covered with the green moss, just a few steps from her stood again The Son of Big Bear. Just the fact that he managed to get so close to her without being noticed shocked her. A minute ago there was not a living creature there, and...well, anyway, it was him, there could be no mistake. Tall with an eagle feather in his hair, stone axe at the belt and leather moccasins. The Son of Big Bear raised his hand to greet her and using sign language he indicated that he was happy to see her. Han-chi did not say a word. The words of Kiwo-to about the Big People were whirling in her head. However, in the end she responded, "What are you doing here? What do you want?"

"I want to get married. I am looking for a squaw. Sawa-Tu-Han-Tala is alone. Sawa-Tu-Han-Tala is a great warrior."

Han-chi's large round eyes became larger and she wondered what would Kiwo-to or Chook-chi say to it. She still didn't know what a warrior was, but somehow it did not bother her anymore. The Son of Big Bear stepped up to the girl, took her hand and tried to explain something to her. By his gestures it looked like he was asking her if she wanted to become his squaw, but then he kept pointing upwards in the direction of the cave. Han-chi became suddenly horrified. This unknown suitor knows about the existence of the cave town and is obviously trying to find out how to get there. Again she heard in her ears Kiwo-to bemoaning the time when the tribe had to flee away from the Big People.

Disclose the way to the cave town? No, she could not do anything like that! She jerked herself free from Son of Big Bear and began to run like a scared deer. This time she would warn the whole tribe. She would tell everybody what kind of a danger they all are in. Son of Big Bear, however, was not willing to give up so easily. In a few leaps he caught up with her, and with threatening gestures tried to tell her that he would kidnap her and then he would find the secret passage to the cave anyway.

He was rolling his beady eyes and all his friendly manners were gone. Then he grabbed her by the hand and dragged her back to the pool. Han-chi, scared to death, began to scream. The rejected suitor did not expect it. He again saw people of his tribe heaping on him scorn and sneers. He had bragged that he would find the passage to the cave town, but now, the Michi-Maki would run away and will take all supplies with them and his tribe would go hungry again. Yeah, really a great scout. What a hero. What a warrior. Suddenly, the notion of instant disgrace coming on him incessantly and from all his friends awakened in him the wild anger of a savage. He raised the axe and tried to scare her into silence, but she, in fear of her life, screamed again. At that moment Son of Big Bear struck her. Han-chi fell silent and her motionless body slid quietly to the ground. At first a small stream of blood appeared, then it slowly wound its way toward the pool and the recently crystal clear water began turning red.

Thirty days later the full moon again flooded the south eastern side of the mesa with the bright light. As the moon continued its journey in the sky, its rays suddenly illuminated a large cave and in it as if covered with silver dust a small town. The dwellings built out of stone were leaning sadly against each other. Total silence reigned in the whole cave. At first glance one would think that all its inhabitants were asleep, but in reality there was not a living soul in the town who could disturb the nightly peace. The town was abandoned. Only rope ladders hanging down into the deep canyon moved silently, as if the spirits were trying to climb up into the cave during the Kiwo-to absence. On this starry night, however, right next to the constellation of the Virgin there shone brightly a new star which at the last full moon was not there.

(Dedicated to the Anasazi, the great builders and peaceful people.)

Historical Notes

Mesa Verde, the national park in southwestern Colorado whose major attraction is the **Cliff Palace** in the story is referred to as a cave town. In a huge rock cavity 324 feet long, 59 feet high and 89 feet long is located an Indian pueblo which was built and populated between 1200 and 1300 A.D. About 200-250 people lived in this cliff dwelling whose culture and language are unknown. After leaving the pueblo these people were absorbed within several generations by the other larger tribes of present-day Arizona and New Mexico. The archeologists call these people **Anasazi** from the Navajo language—**The Ancient Ones**. These pueblo Indians were small in stature and their source of livelihood was predominantly farming, fruit gathering and hunting of small game. They were not aggressive people and their weapons were quite primitive when compared to the neighboring warlike tribes. On the other hand, the perpendicular and often tall walls indicate that they were familiar with basic building techniques and above all with the plumb-line. The reasons for abandoning such pueblos were in the most cases twofold—ongoing drought and arrival of warlike tribes and in this case, the Athabascans, who over the centuries morphed into the current Apache and Navajo tribes. Mesa Verde was discovered by chance by two cowboys—**Richard Wetherill** and **Charles Mason**—on December 18, 1888. The US Congress declared this area an archeological preserve and a National Park in 1906. The first museum was opened there in 1918 by **Dr. Jesse W. Fewkes**. One of the items exhibited for many years was a skull of a young woman that was smashed by a dull object. The cause of her death is matter of pure speculation and the story has offered one option.

Kiva, from the Hopi language, means a ceremonial room.

Yucca is a long leaf plant growing in the arid regions of the American Southwest. Its fiber is suitable for weaving mats, moccasins, baskets, ropes and other useful items.

Pemmican is pulverized dried meat mixed with deer or buffalo tallow. It was the preferred food by the western Indian tribes when traveling because it did not spoil easily.

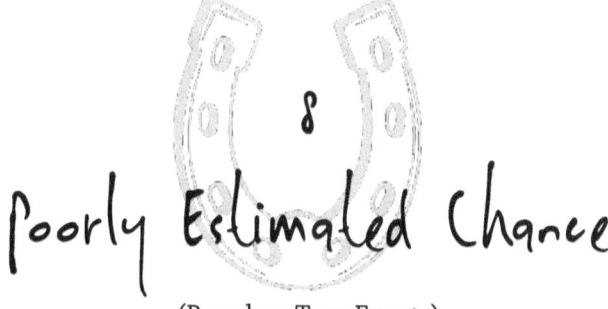

8
Poorly Estimated Chance

(Based on True Events)

The river made an impression that it was fighting this unusual constriction. Its muddy water was suddenly forced into a narrow bed confined on each side by a black granite wall more than two thousand feet high. The river's current accelerated. First, one could hear along the black canyon walls a loud drone of the rushing water which then got louder and louder. After a while, when the river ran into the deep rapids, it turned into a deafening roar. A huge mass of water fell with a thundering noise into a depth of twenty or thirty feet. It kept boiling on the same spot and then madly threw itself against the black boulders and sharp cliffs protruding from the river bottom. They, however, stood motionless, as if they were aware of the fact that no force exists that could move them. Wave after wave harmlessly crashed against them, which turned into the yellowish foam that was splashing several feet high and covered the surrounding rocks. Then, in the middle of the canyon, the water spray formed a grey fog that rose above the rapids and interfered with the view of the lower part of the river.

In a river bend, about two hundred yards above the rapids, a boat suddenly appeared. Already from the distance one could see that it was well built, about sixteen feet long, and it differed from many similar fishing vessels used on American rivers by having not only a bow and a stern, but also a fully covered midsection. Apparently there were food supplies and some equipment which had to be protected from moisture stored in this space. Moreover such a vessel would hardly sink in case of an accident because the covered space would serve as a sort of air pocket which would keep it afloat. There were three men in the boat. One of them stood on the bow attentively watching the river flow in front of him and the other two tried with the help of the oars to slow down the boat which was gaining speed.

The standing man suddenly began waving a red cloth attached to a long stick. He was clearly trying to signal someone. At the same time the rowing men steered the boat toward a sharp upright rock on the left bank. The man on the bow put the signal flag down, unwound a strong hemp rope and threw it around the protruding rock. Judging by the dexterity and efficiency by which he did it, one could come to the conclusion that he was not doing it for the first time. The noose snared up, the rope got taut and the boat stopped with its stern toward the rapids.

A couple of minutes later two other boats pulled up to the first one. These boats were a little bit bigger, at least twenty feet long, and their crews consisted of six men altogether. As soon as they fasten them together and made sure that the strong current would not carry them away, they began to deliberate. Then two men from the first boat stepped on the bank and tried to climb up on a rocky cliff that hindered their view of the rapids. The tall strong guy was helping the other, smaller one who, as one could now see, had only one arm. After a while they managed to climb to the top. From there they studied the rapids and made simple sketches on a piece of paper. Then they climbed down and informed the other six men about what they had seen.

The information about the rapids that they saw in its ominous beauty was not exactly inspiring. The rapids were about three to four hundred yards long and formed two parts. The upper part was almost one hundred feet long and it sloped down sharply so that it resembled a big waterfall. Below it the riverbed flattened a little and on the left side there was a small cove that the river eroded in the canyon wall where one could safely drop the anchor. The lower part of the rapids did not slope as sharply as the upper one, but it was much longer, maybe three or four hundred feet. Boulders and collapsed slabs of granite made passage for any vessel impossible. Perhaps there would be a chance along the right bank. There, it seemed, was enough space for a boat to slip through. What was behind the rapids they could not say, but judging by the geological stratification of the canyon wall the riverbed should be pretty flat and they had the impression that further down the canyon widened. However, one thing was clear. Any attempt to run the rapids would definitely be suicide which meant that the boats had to be lowered by a rope. The rest of the crew would climb down along the bank and would embark in that little cove.

The one-armed man pulled a watch out of his pocket. They had two hours till dusk, so there was no time to waste. Just the notion that they would otherwise spend the night in the swaying boats tied up to a rock less than a hundred yards from the murderous rapids gave them extra energy.

First, they extended the ropes so they could cover the distance of about two hundred yards. Then they tied the rope to an iron ring at the bow of the smaller boat and made sure that all the storage space was shut tight. Finally, the same guy who was helping the one-armed man got into the boat. He had two extra ropes at his feet. One was shorter and tied to an iron hook and the other was longer and attached to an anchor. The one-armed man climbed back to the rocky cliff from where he could see the rapids and the cove and when he gave the signal, seven men, braced with their feet against the slippery rocks, slowly started lowering the man in the boat into the thundering cataract. A few seconds later he disappeared from their sight.

The moment the boat cleared the upper edge of the rapids, the one-armed man saw the trouble. The boat was being lowered too slowly, resisted the current too much and consequently, the waves began to roll over its stern. Moreover, they were tossing the boat from side to side like a cork so there was a real danger that they could upset it and drown its only passenger. The man on the rock immediately realized the problem and with rapid gestures encouraged the other men to lower the boat faster. It worked. The moment they loosened up on the rope, the boat stopped rocking violently, the waves no longer flooded it and a few minutes later he was out of danger. Now he reached for the oars and after some struggle with the current he steered the boat into the cove. There he forced the hook into a crevice in the rock wall and tied up the boat. Then he untied the rope from the iron ring and gave the men on the cliff a signal that they could pull it up.

The other two boats were lowered in the same way. They were empty. As soon as the empty boat reached the foot of the rapids, the man in the cove uncoiled the rope with the anchor and after several attempts hooked it up and pulled it to the bank. Once the second empty boat was safely in the cove, the remaining eight men set out along the rock wall to join their comrade. When they arrived, they again quickly checked the storage bins for leaks or other damage and then took seats at the oars. Some of them also cooled their hands that had been burned by the rope in the muddy water. The most dramatic part of their passage through the rapids was now ahead of them. First they had to cross a relatively safe stretch of the open river, perhaps one hundred feet long. Its lower part, however, was closed by boulders and pointed rocks washed by a strong current. The task of each crew was to get to the other side of the river, reach a narrow channel along the canyon wall and try to safely navigate through it.

The first to set out was the boat with the one-armed man and two men at the oars. The oar men directed the boat toward the foot of the rapids on their right hand side in order not to get swept into the rocks to their left that were ominously protruding from the river bottom like stony knives waiting for the next victim. The men fought the current with all their strength. A few more feet...then, the boat spun to the left and was shooting along the opposite canyon wall. The channel now narrowed down to maybe ten feet. The speed of the boat was increasing. Suddenly, they saw in front of them a boulder almost eight feet high and six feet wide. At the first glance it looked like that it was completely blocking the channel, but when the boat came closer, the oar men saw that to the left of the boulder there was an opening into the middle of the river where they could slip through. They only had to turn the boat sharply to the left. They managed. The boat rubbed its right side against the wet algae-covered wall of the boulder, but the impact was not big and the boat did not upset. After another twenty or thirty yards the river surface calmed down and the rapids were behind them. Then the canyon widened up and in the rock wall on the right there appeared a large opening to a narrow side canyon with a brook on its bottom. Right at the entrance to this canyon they saw a small plateau just a few feet above the river, an ideal place for setting up a camp. The men pulled up to the bank and anxiously waited for the arrival of the next boat.

From this spot they had a clear view of the boulder that was partially blocking the only possible passage through the rapids. Finally on the right side of the boulder in the foaming waves appeared the bow of the second boat and a few minutes later its crew safely landed at the campsite. They also hit the big rock when they were passing it, but they were lucky. Six pairs of eyes tried to penetrate the grey mist above the rapids. Minutes passed, but there was no sign of the third boat. The men became nervous. The canyon was getting dark and if something happened, it could not be at a worse time.

Suddenly, they heard a scream and shortly thereafter they could make out in the distance the bottom of the third boat. At that moment all six men had only one burning question on their minds. Where did they upset it? If it happened in the channel, they have a chance to make it. If it happened before the channel and they got swept up in the rapids, they will probably fish only their dead bodies out of the river. Then the suspense broke. Several yards behind the boat they spotted three bobbing heads. Four men jumped into the bigger boat, leaned on the oars and after a while they pulled the unlucky crew and their boat to the safety. The rescued men then described what happened. While going through the channel, they broke one oar and before they managed to put in a spare one, they saw that damn boulder. There they lost control over the boat and even though they managed to avoid directly hitting it, they could not prevent the boat from tipping over. Except for a few scratches, they are okay.

Who were these people who were passing through this hell? During the day they have to cope with deadly heat and at night they fought the chill. They could see the sun only two or three hours a day, depending on how wide the particular part of the canyon that they happen to be going through was. Practically every day they dragged the heavy oak boats and lowered them through the rapids that were created by the devil himself. Most of the time they slept on the rocks or in the boats tied to a rock wall.

Well, let me introduce them to you. The one-armed man was Major John Wesley Powell, a veteran of the Civil War, and by profession a land surveyor and geologist. He managed to convince several Midwestern universities to finance an expedition whose purpose was to map the still unknown territory along the Colorado River in the southern part of Utah and northern part of Arizona. He was accompanied by eight volunteers: J. C. Sumner, a man with great sense for adventure and a enthusiastic hunter, W. H. Powell, the major's brother and an artillery captain, William H. Dunn a hunter and trapper, G.Y. Bradley a sergeant in the US Army, Captain O. G. Howland, a printer and newsman by profession, his brother Seneca Howland, W. R. Hawkins a hunter and trapper and finally Andrew Hall, also a hunter and trapper. All of them except Hall, Seneca, Howland and Dunn were veterans who served in the Union Army.

Shortly after the landing at the stony plateau the men made a camp fire. They managed to collect enough dry wood in the side canyon and now the flames pushed back a little of the pitch black darkness and helped dry the clothes of the crew who got spilled out. The others worked on a modest supper. It was truly modest because the food supplies were rapidly disappearing. The bacon, sugar and beans were gone, only coffee and some flour was left. And the flour was less than what was needed for the rest of the trip. Due to ever present dampness it was getting mildew and had to be sifted so now they were running out of it.

After dinner Captain Howland asked the Major for a private conversation.

Both men walked a short distance from the campfire, sat down on the rocks near the brook and quietly spoke. After a while they returned and rejoined the others. Everybody sat quietly around the fire and the silence was interrupted only by the cracking of the burning wood. The Major kept looking into the dancing flames and did not say anything. The other men glanced at him curiously, sensing that he was going to announce something serious. Finally, he raised his head, looked at the others and slowly, as if weighing every word, he said, "I never thought that something like this would happen during our trip, but I see I was mistaken. Captain Howland told me a while ago his decision to leave the expedition. His brother Seneca and Bill Dunn will join him."

The Major's announcement was followed by a grave like silence. The three men whose intentions were revealed looked to the ground as if they were now ashamed for their decision. The others were speechless, because they would not have expected something like this happened. True, they were running out of the supplies, that's true, but the situation was not yet so tragic that they would have to abort the expedition. Major Powell cleared his throat and continued, "Since this is a civilian project and not a military one, I cannot force anyone to stay. In other words, if most of you decide to quit, then we'll all return. Therefore I suggest we discuss all aspects, consider all facts and then vote. In the case most of you support the decision of Captain Howland then we'll pull the boats on the bank and start the trip back by land."

After the Major's announcement a lively debate ensued. Captain Howland insisted that to keep continuing the trip was a sheer madness. The provisions would last two or three more days, but they might be traveling another two or three weeks. Major Powell stuck to his calculations according to which the end of the Grand Canyon was within a two or three day reach. Seneca Howland, the Captain's brother, did not try to hide his mistrust of these calculations, because the sextant and other equipment used to establish their location are in such a poor shape that they could not rely on them. Bill Dunn argued that with the existing supplies they could make it to the Mormon settlements because traveling overland would not be so exacting. Over how many more rapids did the major believe they would be able to drag the boats while being hungry and weak?

Captain Howland then described the overland route as a trip through paradise compared to what is waiting for them in the canyon. They could hunt along the way, and if it got hot, they would travel only at night and they will rest during the day. The Major warned them that they were not choosing between hell and paradise, but rather between a greater and lesser evil. He, who was familiar with southern Utah, tried to explain to them that what was waiting for them up there was unknown terrain, open desert without water and shade, heat like in hell and one hundred fifty miles to the nearest town. Here, in the canyon, there at least was water and at night it cooled off. Then he added that to give up after all the hardship they went through and the struggle with the canyon, it would mean to admit defeat. Seneca then remarked that he would prefer to stay alive and be able to admit defeat rather than to die just before reaching the goal. The men kept arguing for a while, but it seemed that Captain Howland, his brother and Bill Dunn had made up their minds. The Major then asked for a vote. Who would prefer to abort the expedition? Only three hands went up.

The Major fell asleep only toward morning. He reproached himself the whole night for not being able to dissuade those three from their intentions. Even though they decided to leave the expedition by their own volition, he still, as main organizer of this project, felt responsible for them. He felt horrified by the naïve ideas they had about the land along the northern rim of the canyon.

They parted after breakfast. The remaining provisions were evenly divided and in addition to the flour and coffee, Captain Howland received for himself and his companions three rifles and a handful of ammunition. Major Powell wrote a few lines for his wife and asked the captain to take with him the copy of the notes describing the course of the whole expedition. While saying goodbye he tried again to persuade them to reconsider, but to no avail. The other men then pulled out the smaller boat on the plateau just in case those three changed their minds and returned. The last farewell and two boats, each with a three men crew, pushed away and after a while disappeared in the river bend.

The three men left behind picked up the rifles and set out along the brook into the narrow canyon. After several minutes of a brusque walk the canyon widened and the black granite walls changed into brown and yellow cliffs with eroded dirt at their feet. In some spots one could even detect sage and dwarf pines. The captain then expressed the opinion that if the terrain did not change they could reach the top of the canyon by noon. The ground really did not change that much, but complications of a different kind emerged. The canyon started to break up into a number of smaller canyons and glens which in most case ended in a steep several hundred foot tall rock wall. Then they had to retrace their steps and try their luck in a different direction. Only toward evening did they managed to extricate themselves from this natural maze and reach the northern rim of the Grand Canyon

Dead tired and hungry they collapsed under the first big pine tree and took a quick glance toward the river which, of course, they no longer could see. The setting sun illuminated the jagged walls of the canyon and flooded them with a spectrum of bright colors and dark shadows. The canyon, as if it wanted to give them a farewell present, prepared a sight which an average mortal can see only rarely. The men, swept away by this fantastic natural phenomenon, were speechless. They just wished at the bottom of their hearts that the others were present and could share this amazing show with them. Yes, the others who were probably right now struggling somewhere with the rapids or were trying to find a safe place where they could spend the night. After a while of silence the men got up and began to scout the terrain. They were pleasantly surprised when they found out that they were at the edge of a pine forest stretching not only for several miles along the rim but also inland. Captain Howland then decided to camp about a mile away from the canyon because they would be better protected against the storm which soaked them practically every day. There was also a chance that deeper in the woods they could shoot a deer or a rabbit. After many weeks they would finally eat their fill.

Shortly after sunrise Bill Dunn set out to hunt. When he returned, the sun was already beating into the green tops of the trees and the hot air was replacing the night cool. Both brothers rushed toward him expecting that they would have venison or at least a rabbit roast for breakfast, but Bill returned empty handed. Not only did he not see a living creature, but he made it all the way to the end of the forest and there...there really started the desert. Yesterday when they scrambled out of the canyon and saw the forest, they all agreed that the Major was damn mistaken when he painted the landscape between the Grand Canyon and the Mormon settlements in such gloomy colors, but now uncertainty started taking over. What if he was right after all? As soon as they finished a modest breakfast that consisted of a few flat cakes and cups of coffee, they packed the blankets and headed north. About a half an hour later the trees spread out and they entered into an endless dust desert. There was not a sign of life anywhere and only in the far distance in the hot quivering air could they see a bluish mountain range. A thought crossed Captain Howland's mind that the morning's coffee had been made from the last of the drinking water they had carried from the canyon. If there was water anywhere, it would be in those hills and they were at least ten or twelve fast walking hours away. After a short debate they decided not to wait for the evening and from the pleasant cool of the forest they stepped out on the sun baked plain.

At first they were moving rather quickly. They were rested and the terrain was table flat. In the afternoon, however, thirst started to take its toll. The clenching feeling of fatigue and stupor turned into a dull pain. The sun not only burned their bare heads, they had lost their hats long time before in the canyon, andt the dry desert air drew every drop of liquid out of their bodies. The men had stopped perspiring because the hot dry air evaporated the tiny droplets of sweat before they reached the skin's surface. Only little crystals of salt formed around their eyes. They slowly shuffled forward and had a strange feeling that the blue hills ahead kept retreating from them. Now they had to stop and rest more often. The Captain's brother Seneca suffered most. He was a blond guy and his light complexion soon succumbed to the attack of the burning sun. Blister after blister began to cover his face, and then within a few minutes they dried up and became bloody scabs.

Only at sunset did it seem that the mountain range was within reach. Seneca, however, was at the end of his strength. His brother and Bill Dunn tried to support him from both sides, but eventually they all sat down, completely exhausted. They turned their backs toward the setting sun and in silence stared into the grey dust. Were they going to end up the way the Major told them? He and the others now struggled somewhere with the rapids to fight for their life but us? Seneca wanted to laugh hysterically, but only a muffled sound came out of his parched mouth. He suddenly imagined the quantity of water flowing by their boats. A sea of water, millions of gallons of water, and they... All riches of the world they would give for a drop of water. No one spoke. They were tired and their dehydrated throats could not produce understandable speech anyway. Their eyelids began to close and all they wanted was to sleep. The feeling of pain and thirst was mercifully getting weaker. Just close the eyes, forget all this suffering and go to sleep. Suddenly, they no longer worried how far the mountains or the Mormon settlements were. Who cares now? Just lie down, fall asleep and don't wake up.

At this moment, tortured by thirst and heat as they began to succumb to the mortal lethargy, a long shadow fell in front of them. Bill Dunn, who still kept his head somewhat clear, believed that it was a mirage caused by an overtaxed brain. Nevertheless, he slowly turned around and raised his head. Several feet away stood a half-naked Indian curiously looking at them. In one hand he held a bow and in the other an arrow ready to put on the string. Bill slowly raised his hand to greet him and using the sign language signaled that they meant no harm. The Indian put the arrow carefully in the quiver made out of yucca fiber and raised both hands, also indicating that he came in peace. Bill then handed over to him his flask and again using the sign language tried to explain that they were dying of thirst. The Indian inquisitively observed all three of them for about a minute, then reached to his waist, untied a small clay bottle and poured a little water into Bill's flask. Then again using sign language he tried to explain something to him, but Bill did not understand. For God's sake, what did he want? Why doesn't he give me the flask? Then he finally understood. The Indian was telling him that he had water only for one man, the strongest one. He must take the other flasks and follow him. There was a spring in the mountains, about one hour of walking. There he would fill the flasks and return to his friends. Bill nodded his head, poured just one gulp in a little metal cup for the Captain and one gulp for his brother. He then assured them that he would be back as soon as possible. He then drank up the rest of water in his flask, rose to his feet and followed the Indian who headed toward the foothills.

The Indian was right. After about an hour of walking they entered a wide canyon. It was getting dark when the Indian guide stopped and pointed to a rock wall. Bill could not believe his eyes. About three feet above the ground was a narrow stream of cold water flowing out of a rocky crevice. Had he come here alone, he would probably never have found it. Bill did not waste any time. He knelt at the stream and drank with long gulps straight from the crevice. Water was flowing all over his face and pleasantly cooling his burning cheeks. After a while the mortifying fatigue was gone and so was the pain in his gut. He quickly filled all three flasks and turned around to thank the strange rescuer, but he had disappeared as if he had vanished into thin air. Bill shrugged his shoulders and set out on the way back to his friends.

Shortly after midnight all three were sitting around a camp fire not far from the life saving spring and consuming the last of the flat cakes made out of rye flour. Right now they all felt good. They had managed to quench their thirst and hunger and the fact that they escaped the trap set up by the merciless desert somehow built up their confidence. That Indian was a true act of Providence because he showed up really at five minutes to twelve. If the Indians could survive here, why couldn't they? Captain Howland then sarcastically remarked that if he were certain that the same Indian would show up again tomorrow with a bowl of flat cakes and a pot of black coffee, he would feel much better, but right now it was a little bit too early to rejoice. While they were wondering what the next day would bring, the campfire suddenly threw light on a silhouette of man. He appeared so silently and so suddenly that they did not even have the time to reach for their rifles. To their great astonishment it was the very same Indian who brought Bill Dunn to this spring. Without saying a word he placed in front of each man a roasted corn ear, then squatted and watched the men who were so surprised that they didn't know what to say. Bill, who was a little bit more conversant as to the sign language than his comrades, began to "chat" with this mysterious visitor, and after a while he grasped the true purpose of his nightly visit. Further up the canyon there was an Indian pueblo and the chief would like to have the honor of welcoming them to his village.

The whole pueblo, including its inhabitants, made an unmistakable impression that this tribe was quite poor. The main sources of their livelihood were pinon nuts picked in the woods and corn or beans raised in small fields. Maybe hunters sometimes brought in a deer or a mountain goat, but the absence of skins drying in the sun suggested that it did not happen too often. The dwellings were mostly simple stone and mud huts spread randomly along the canyon walls. The chief was an old white-haired man wearing torn up pants out of homespun fabric that had gotten into his possession in some mysterious way. He sat on a mat woven out of yucca fiber and smoked peacefully from a clay pipe as his eyes squinted because of the morning sun. When the three white men accompanied by the Indian emissary arrived, he welcomed them with a friendly gesture, had another three mats brought next to his and motioned the visitors to sit down. The rest of the villagers made a circle and from a polite distance ogled the strangers. The chief was already familiar with yesterday's events and that's why he was mainly interested where they had come from. The conversation was carried out again by sign language, broken English and occasionally one could hear a Spanish word. From this talk one could conclude that these Indians had some contact with white men, primarily with the Mormon missionaries who tried to convert them to their religion. Captain Howland tried to explain that they had come from the East, that they had floated down the river and had walked out of the Great Canyon, but the chief only shook his head incredulously and kept repeating, "Cross canyon—yes. Go on river—not possible. Heap of wild water. Nobody remembers."

Captain Howland realized that he could not convince the chief and so he let him have his doubts and began asking how far it is to the Mormon settle-ments. The chief nodded his head, pointed at the rocky hills and raised three fingers. "Three day in shadow of mountain. Then river." He bent, drew a line in the sand and raised two fingers. "Two day against river." Finally the captain carefully asked if they could supply them with food for at least three days before they could get to the river. The chief readily answered that they were a poor tribe and that last year's crop was not too good and that he had to consult the elders. Several older Indians joined the chief and they began deliberating. Then the captain got the idea that it wouldn't hurt to motivate the chief a little bit. He pulled out of his vest a silver a pocket watch and by a gesture indicated that he was willing to exchange this ticking miracle for a pile of ears of corn or beans. To his great astonishment the chief refused the offer and announced that each man will get ten corn ears and two handfuls of beans. Then he added that his tribe was happy to help the white men because it wanted to live with them in peace and friendship. Shortly after lunch all three men carrying the newly obtained provisions and wearing hats made out of yucca on their heads left the pueblo and headed north.

About two hours passed. The Indians dispersed and only the chief and a few old men kept rehashing the recent visit by the three strangers, who so unexpectedly appeared as if they had fallen from the sky. However, fate did not intend to let them return to their daily routine so quickly. A messenger from the neighboring tribe living on the other side of the Grand Canyon arrived and brought news that caused excitement in the whole pueblo. Uwi-ha, a young Indian woman was returning home with her son when she saw a campfire. Being too curious for her own good she went closer to see who was camping there. What happened next we know only from her son. Three white men crazed by firewater knocked her down and tore her clothes off. Uwi-ha screamed and the boy ran away. When he brought the warriors to the place, the fire was still burning, but the men were gone and Uwi-ha lay dead on the ground with her head smashed. Their tracks led to the Grand Canyon. If you see these three men, avenge her spilled blood!

The chief again called the elders. He could not believe that those three who behaved so friendly could have been the killers. On the other hand their story about passing through the Grand Canyon...? The messenger repeated again the tragic story and when he heard that three white men passed through the pueblo just a couple of hours ago, he threw himself on the ground and began to wail and bemoan the murdered Uwi-ha. Then he got up and delivered a rousing speech,

"White men keep killing our women and children. They murder them with their fiery arms. They don't spare anyone. The red people don't want war, they want to live in peace, but still no Indian can be sure what will happen if he runs into a white man. Who will bury the dead when the last Indian is killed? The white men must not think that the Indians are cowards and that they will keep on running and hiding!" Finally he used the strongest argument, "How can you believe the fairytale about their passage through the Grand Canyon? Or perhaps are your warriors afraid of three cowardly dogs that kill defenseless squaws?" The last sentence had the decisive effect. They were not warlike people, but they were not cowards either, and so the approving muttering of the elders calling for revenge drowned the chief's doubts.

The mood around the campfire was upbeat. Seneca sat on the ground with his back against a rock wall while scooping with his left hand rain water from a little pool and cooling his face. The burns he suffered when crossing the desert had begun to heal and thanks to the yucca hats no new ones appeared. His brother, Captain Howland, was cleaning his rifle and at the same time expressing his thoughts, "It was a damn good decision to leave the expedition. Those poor devils have snowballs chance in hell to come out of the canyon alive. They certainly don't have lack of water, but we don't either. Also look at all that food!" and with great relish bit into a freshly roasted corn ear. "I'll be damned if Bill sooner or later doesn't shoot something that will taste like meat. We'll cook a cup of beans to go with it and then feast like kings. Once we reach the river, we'll have made it. At worst, we can always catch some fish and we'll be fine. No, I'll tell you, the Major made a mistake. I wouldn't give a stick of chewing tobacco for their lives. The trouble is that Powell wants to be famous, and now it may cost him his life." The captain went on reflecting about their and Major Powell's situation, but it was basically a monologue because Dunn dozed off and Seneca just did not pay much attention.

Then suddenly, in the pitch black darkness was heard a rattling noise of a loosened stone. Bill Dunn woke up and believing that it was an animal attracted by the fire, reached for the rifle. At that moment the silence was broken by an unpleasant sound with which all settlers were quite familiar, the hissing sound of an arrow.

The train started moving slowly. Major Powell sank into the comfortable seat of the first class compartment of a big Pullman, lit up a cigar and looking out of the window caught the sight of a large sign saying CHICAGO - THE MAIN STATION. Then he reached into his pocket, pulled out the local newspaper and glanced over the splash headlines announcing the success of his expedition: *Major Powell Solved the Mystery of the Grand Canyon, The Midsection of the Colorado River Finally Mapped, Six Brave Men survived the Hell of the Grand Canyon. Where Are the Other Three?*

Right, sighed the major, where are the other three? This question bothered him from Salt Lake City all the way here to Chicago. He spent almost a week at the local university sorting his notes and giving several lectures, but there was no news about those three as if they had vanished into the thin air. He sent cables to the fort commanders in Utah, Colorado and Wyoming, but none of them had a clue. Suddenly, somebody knocked on the door. The Major said "Come in" and the train conductor entered. He apologized for disturbing the passenger, but then explained that he had just received a telegram addressed to Major Powell and that's why he immediately brought it in. The Major looked at the envelope and held his breath. The telegram was sent from Salt Lake City. He quickly opened it and his eyes read the following lines:

The bodies of three men full of arrows were found about ten miles from an Indian pueblo in the southern part of Utah. Materials discovered indicate that the men in question were members of Major Powell's expedition.

Historical Notes

John Wesley Powell, a one-armed major, and eight other volunteers entered the history of geological exploration because they were the first white men who succeeded in passing through the Grand Canyon, mapping the adjacent area and by such an act permanently remaining the last spot on the map of the United State which was marked "Hic sunt leones." Major J. W. Powell was born in 1834 in Mount Morris New York, and after having finished high school he studied geology at Wheaton and Oberlin Universities. During the Civil War he served in the Union Army with the rank of Major. During the battle of **Shiloh** (Tennessee) in 1862 a bullet shattered his right arm which had to be amputated below the shoulder. After the war he returned to his favorite subject, geology, on which he lectured at Wesley University in Illinois. As to geological exploration, he was attracted primarily by the arid regions of the Southwest, partly because this area was little known and partly because from a geological point of view it was unique. In the year 1868 he decided to organize an expedition which would gain factual information about this region not only as to geology but also ethnography. In addition to the financial support of the Illinois Industrial University and Illinois Historical Society he also secured the strong support of his former military commander, at that time the President of the United States, **Ulysses S. Grant**. Grant offered food supplies for twelve men or money in that value. Powell preferred money. The **Smithsonian Institution** also lent Powell a number of instruments necessary for establishing their location and creating a reliable chart of the area they planned to go through. However, the greater part of the cost was covered by the major himself. He believed that upon successfully completing this exploration he would recover the invested capital in the form of lectures and articles for scientific magazines. Powell and nine volunteers traveled by railroad to the town of **Green River City** in Utah with provisions, measuring instruments and four boats. Here the railroad crosses the **Green River**. From there on May 24 the expedition set out on a trip almost 1000 miles long that lasted 98 days. The expedition followed the Green River all the way to the **Grand River** which then flowed into the **Colorado River**. Only in 1921 was it decided that the Colorado River has its springs in the state of Colorado and so the Grand River was renamed the Colorado River.

Powell's expedition had to face many difficulties and overcome many obstacles. It was not only the rapids and an unknown wild river but also the shortage of food and psychological stress. For example, shortly after their departure from Green River City, thanks to inexperience of the oar men, the crew F. Goodman, Captain Howland and his brother Seneca broke their boat "No Name" into pieces in the Lodore Canyon. After this bitter experience Major Powell decided to no longer take any risks and the boats were transported through the rapids with the help of ropes. During the trip Powell and the others charted the direction of the river, marked on the map the side canyons and measured the height of the canyon walls. They also found at several places Indian dwellings abandoned more than a thousand years ago, pictographs and petroglyphs. Before the confluence of the Green and Grand Rivers F. Goodman, an English adventurer, came to the conclusion that he had enough of the adventure and abandoned the expedition. He remained on the Ute reservation and later on made it safely back to the East. The overall mood of the travelers got worse during the passage through the Grand Canyon due to an increasing amount of rapids, diminishing food supplies, and the fact that the river turned south. It meant they were getting farther away from the Mormon settlements where the expedition planned to arrive. The last factor forced Captain Howland, his brother Seneca and Bill Dunn to leave the expedition because they were convinced that to keep on going would mean certain death. (The place where they split is called **The Separation Canyon**.) It would be hard to find in the history of exploration a greater irony. Major Powell and the rest of the expedition floated out of the Grand Canyon several days later and near the mouth of the **Virgin River** they ran into a man and a boy who were fishing there. These two told them that they were only twenty miles away from the nearest town called **Calville**. In other words, Powell's calculations were correct. The group led by Captain Howland, hungry and almost dying of thirst, ran into the Shivwitz Indians who provided them with food and sent them in the right direction of the Mormon settlements. Shortly after their departure an Indian (either Hualapai or Hawasupai) arrived from the other side of the Grand Canyon with the news about three prospectors who while drunk had raped and killed a young Indian woman. Since the majority of the Indians did not believe Captain Howland that they passed through the Grand Canyon, it did not take long to convince the Shivwitz that those three white men were the killers.

Major Powell retuned to this region a year later, he traveling through the canyon again, but this time he was better equipped and also conducted a broader exploration of the area bordering on the canyon. On this occasion he met with the Shivwitz Indians who told him the story about the prospectors. However, Powell tactfully concealed the fact that they had actually killed his own men.

Even though the exploration of the Grand Canyon made Major Powell very popular, the center of his contributions to the American society lies somewhere else. First, we have to mention the fact that he founded **The United States Geological Survey** and later on became one of the co-founders of an important cultural organization, **The National Geographic Society** whose monthly *The National Geographic Magazine* is one of the most popular publications in the world. Powell further contributed to ethnological studies among the local Indians, particularly as to understanding their culture and languages, and he deserves major credit for the compilation of a lot of information that became useful to the American government later on during the political and economic development of this region. Major John Wesley Powell died in the town of Haven, Maine on September 23, 1902.

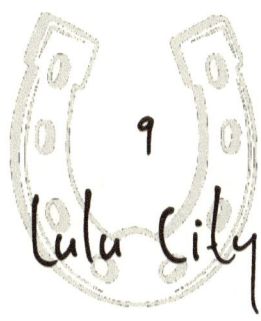

9
Lulu City

An older man appeared on a trail winding along a rock wall. It seemed at first glance that he was a trapper who wanted to try his luck near the beaver dams in the upper part of the Grand River, but a local would quickly reject such a notion. The worn out denim pants and fur vest made the impression that this person didn't have much contact with civilization, but the solid leather boots suggested that he was a man who moved in mountainous rocky terrain and who did not care whether his walk was noisy or not. A trapper whose livelihood depends on how quietly he can travel through the woods would definitely prefer soft Indian moccasins. The man was a little over five feet tall, his thick wavy beard was pretty grey and the hair flowing down to his shoulders had not been in contact with scissors for many months. Judging by his wrinkled face he was over sixty years old. He walked slowly, slightly bent forward, and his right hand was leading a small grey donkey. The items the donkey carried on its back left no doubts—this old man was a prospector.

On a carefully fitted pack saddle one could see a shining pan, pick, shovel, wooden box for ore samples and the complete camping equipment of a man who has to spend months without a roof over his head and at the mercy of the weather. The trail rose sharply toward a saddle where it leveled off providing a magnificent view of mountain glaciers. Here Mike, the name of the old man, stopped for a while to catch his breath because it is not that easy to breathe at an elevation of ten thousand feet. All red in the face, he took off his fur hat and wiped his forehead. Even though it was mid October and the temperature hovered at forty degrees, crossing the Continental Divide made him pretty sweaty. He leaned against the donkey, looked around and it occurred to him that when he passed through here in the spring at one spot there was a waterfall turning into a creek. Now the waterfall as well the creek was gone and instead there was just a solid sheet of ice. He scratched the donkey's ears and, as most do people living alone, he expressed his thoughts aloud. He did it either for himself or for his four-legged companion Jamie.

"This year the winter came kind of early, huh?" Jamie only pricked up his ears and looked around to see if he could find a little bit of grass. His thick coat, however, confirmed the old man's words. Heavy clouds parted and the sun shone on the eastern side of the Rocky Mountains. It was a great sight. The mountain peaks covered by the glaciers and snow glistened in dazzling white; the rich green of pines, spruces and firs in the valley created a giant natural carpet and the deep blue sky completed the picture of an amazingly beautiful landscape. Looking west into the valley one could see the bluish surface of Bear Lake and like a glittering silver thread the Bear River which flows out of it.

"Let's take a breather," said Mike as he threw the rope over the donkey's neck and tied it to the pack saddle. He let Jamie study the remnants of grass peeking through the snowy dust along the trail. Mike knew that when Jamie was carrying his load, he would not go anywhere. Then he sat down on a grey rock and again looked in the valley toward Bear Lake. Down there at the foot of the Continental Divide he spent practically the whole summer. First, he looked for gold along the Thomson River. It was in May, and there was snow still in many places, but he had the itch to go. He waded through the snow drifts along its banks and submerged the pan in ice cold water scooping sand or gravel, but no color. Then he followed the river to its springs, but got the same results.

When he returned, he checked out the dirt along the rocks because he knew that over the years the rivers changed their beds, so there was a possibility that some gold could be placed in just plain dirt, but all was in vain. It was the beginning of August when he was back at Bear Lake. Here he decided to set up a temporary camp. He cut a pile of young firs, built five foot tall walls and erected a tent over them. From the remaining logs he made a little table and a chair and stuffed a big sack with grass so he would finally sleep in comfort. In this way he could prospect in the area, particularly along the Bear River, and in the evening return to a dry and cozy abode.

At the beginning it looked promising. At the upper section of the river he panned out a few grains of gold, but then luck left him. He tried the other side of the river, but the results were again quite meager. He stood the whole day in ice cold water and by evening he had gold dust worth maybe five dollars. No big deal.

Then it happened like a miracle! It was at the beginning of September. It was getting cold and Mike was seriously considering packing everything and going back to Great Lake. One morning he got up and...what the hell...Jamie was gone! It was the last thing he needed. He cursed all donkeys, including their parents, and especially those which knew how to get untied, and set out to look for him. The hoof prints led him to the right bank of the Bear River and then downstream. Jamie must have left the camp pretty early because after two hours of calling and fighting with the underbrush there was no sign of him. Only the tracks in the wet soil and piles of donkey droppings indicated that Mike was going in the right direction. Finally, the forest thinned out and Mike saw a small clearing with high grass.

"That darn critter should be here somewhere," he said and kept looking in all directions hoping to catch a glimpse of the long donkey's ears with tufts of black hair on the top of them protruding from tall grass. Jamie's tracks led straight to the river. "He couldn't go for a swim. The water is ice cold, but..." Mike did not finish his thought. On the other side of the river, just a few steps from the bank stood Jamie. As a true connoisseur he rubbed his neck against a trunk of a dead pine and then to maximize his donkey's bliss he raised his hind leg and scratched couple of times behind his big ear. Under different circumstances he would respond to Mike's calling, but since his belly was full, he acknowledged his presence and with donkey-like stoicism waited until Mike crossed the river and they could head back to the lake.

When Mike finally made it to the other side and snapped the rope on Jamie's halter, he noticed that his hooves were covered with light mud and... wait a minute, mud does not shine like this. He squatted on to his front left foot, wiped off the mixture of sand and clay with his palm and for a moment became stupefied. Not only small grains of gold but even a few little nuggets glittered in his hand. Mike felt almost dizzy. There was on Jamie's one hoof gold worth at least ten dollars. Well, it was not the first time he discovered a deposit of gold or a silver vein, but in such concentration? It's a mother lode! All excited he jumped up, embraced the donkey's neck and began to kiss Jamie on his nose, pull his long ears and choked by a feeling of indescribable happiness, tried to explain to him what this discovery meant. Jamie probably thought that all that traipsing in the mountains and poking in the dirt made the old man finally go nuts, but since he was basically a good natured creature, he put up with it.

In six weeks Mike extracted gold valued at almost of two thousand dollars, and that was just by panning. He had not started to dig yet. Well, that would be too much for him; he just could not cut it anymore, but if he could get a partner in Lulu City, then...Mike just sighed. Twice in his life he thought he had gold luck firmly in his hand. In 1862 in Virginia City, Nevada he discovered gold nuggets near the Comstock Lode. He started to push a shaft straight into the bedrock. The sandstone quickly yielded to his pick and when he was fifty feet deep, the digging produced almost a hundred dollars a day. Then the sandstone disappeared and instead of it he hit loose gravel and that was the beginning of the end. When the first landslide happened, he was really lucky.

He sat in the Silver Horseshoe Saloon drinking whisky when the other miners heard a noise in his mine and they brought the news that the entrance was clouded with dust. Well, Mike did not give up. This mine was too good to leave it just because of one mishap. He spent the whole week cleaning and hauling out the debris. He again timbered the whole tunnel and kept on mining. However, this time, he timbered more often and more thoroughly and slowly. He was getting such a good feeling that he had beaten the bad luck. Then, about a month later, the damn tunnel collapsed again. This time he almost did not make it. It took a couple of the fellow miners two hours to pull him out and his left leg was in pretty bad shape and he couldn't walk for almost another month. Then the experts came, looked at the local mines and the rock of the tunnel walls and came to a definite conclusion. Normal timbering won't hold the rock. Due to the geological makeup of the Eastern side of the Sierras it was necessary to use trussing...and that the little guys could not afford. Within a short period of time several banks from San Francisco purchased all the claims and it didn't take long until one of the richest and most productive mines in the Comstock area came into being—the mine Ophir.

Then what? Well, then nothing for quite a while. He tried it in Colorado near Pikes Peak, but that wasn't worth a damn. He barely made enough money for food and had to do grub prospecting. However, in 1874, in the Black Hills of the Dakotas, the streak of bad luck broke. He found a good placer lode in Spring Creek near Hill City and so he set to work right away. He dug up a shaft almost twenty feet deep and braced it well to prevent its walls from collapsing. Then he erected a winch over the pit and a rocker with the sluice on the creek's bank to separate gold dust from the dirt. He spent one day digging at the bottom of the shaft and hauling the gold rich dirt to the top. He spent the next day working the rocker and storing the gold dust in small linen pouches or empty whisky bottles. It worked smoothly without a hitch, except for one small detail.

That year the summer was pretty dry and by the end of August he could cross Spring Creek without getting his feet wet. Needless to say, a rocker needs hundreds of gallons of water a day, but water was getting scarce. By that time quite a number of people were mining along Spring Creek and one of them was a German fellow called Steinhof. When Steinhof saw that all their effort could fail just because of lack of water, he came with the idea to dam that darn creek about a half mile above the mines. He used to help build ponds where he was born, so he was good at it. To dam a creek like Spring Creek would be a piece of cake. So everybody quit digging in their mines and the whole bunch of miners rushed to build this useful water work. They dragged rocks and tree trunks from the nearby woods, drove pillars into the creek's bottom and when they were done, there was a pretty decent lake spreading behind the simple dam with a water gate. When the rockers were still, the water gate was shut tight, then the gate got open a little and the rockers were working non-stop. Everybody felt great and they almost built Steinhof a monument.

Well, those days Mike was positive that had made it. No need to worry about the landslides and expensive timbering. All he had to do was to work hard with the shovel and the pick and then the next days the rocker was full of grains and fine scales of gold. However, there is the unwritten rule, that one extreme follows the other. The summer was dry, but during the winter there was record snowfall. Spring came early and it was unusually warm. The moment the snow on the mountain slopes began to melt, there was trouble lurking round the corner. The mountain freshets turned into rivers and those were taking anything that was in their way. In Spring Creek's way was Steinhof's dam. It defied the rushing water for several days, but when it finally gave way, the destructive current swept away all the rockers, flooded the shafts dug out with so much work and in the end it almost killed some people in the mining camp in the valley. The poor guy Steinhof saved his life only because he fled not only from high water, but also from the ungrateful miners who wanted to lynch him. If he had not come up with this devilish idea, such a disaster would not have happened.

Mike now interrupted his thoughts, got up from the rock and rubbed his left leg to suppress the pain, a reminder of the old injury from Comstock. He looked around to see what Jamie was doing, but Jamie was struggling with a little bush near the trail and the only thing that was on his mind was to pick all those few leaves which the fall winds had not yet knocked down. Mike stepped up to him, took the rope in his hand and led him back to the trail. Then he checked the pack saddle and slowly began walking. The donkey looked sadly back at the bush where a few leaves remained and trotted along. After a while a breathtaking view of the eastern part of the divide opened up. One could see the valley of the Grand River including the Grand Lake which the river formed. The valley was confined on both sides by high snow-covered peaks and at the foot of the tallest one, in a flood of gold-like yellow aspens one could discern small black dots.

It was Lulu City, a new gold mining town founded near the springs of the Grand River. Lulu City was Mike's second home. For the past four years he spent every winter here. At a downtown hotel owned by a well preserved widow of a Montana rancher, he had a room reserved from fall till spring, and moreover Miss Lily, as everybody called the hotel owner, kept his large wooden trunk which contained all his worldly possessions—a black woolen suit, which he put on when he spent an evening in The Queen of Spades Saloon, a couple of white shirts, warm boots lined with sheepskin, a handful of old photographs and yellow newspaper clippings. Just looking at the distant town Mike's face brightened up. The old man began talking again. Of course the dwarfed mountain pines and Jamie were his only audience, but he did not mind.

"Jamie, do you see those black dots down there? That's our home. Now this time, I'll put you in the roomiest stall. Last year I cheated you a little in oats, but this winter it will be different. I bet you old Pete won't believe his ears when I pour a little bit of gold dust in his palm and tell him—Pete, this year only the best for Jamie. Oats twice a day, proper bedding and regular brushing. He'll wonder what happened. Then I'll stop at O'Brien's to get a haircut and a shave and then straight to the hotel. Miss Lily will be surprised because she is expecting me a couple of weeks later, but that will be all right. She will send Mary upstairs to my room to make it ready and then I'll put on my Sunday suit and quick to The Queen of Spades. There we'll whoop it up. I know the regulars will be full of fun. When they see me, they'll holler—Mike is here! The "washed out" Mike. We will have to celebrate! You know, those sons of a gun call me that way because of the flooding at Spring Creek, but I'll respond—You dust-eaters, how many tunnels collapsed on you? Then I'll tell cross-eyed Jack, he is the barkeep there, you know—The best whisky for everybody and things start swinging pretty quickly." Mike jerked the rope. "Come on, Jamie! Move! It's at least another fifteen miles. It's downhill all the way, so we could be there before dusk."

The vision of a red hot oven in the corner of the saloon where he would warm up his old bones and the notion of the excitement his arrival would cause gave somehow his rheumatic legs extra strength. "You would not believe," Mike continued his monologue, "what kind of interesting company is there. Let's take for example the Doc. He is a strange bird. He sits the whole evening at the table, doesn't say much and once a while coughs a little bit. He keeps cards in his hand and anybody who has got some dough can play poker with him. I never saw him lose. They say that he is a dentist, but he wouldn't even think about opening an office. Or take Trapper. He is a big man, tall like a hickory. He used to trap beaver all over the Northwest. Do you know what they say about him?" Mike looked around as if he wanted to make sure that nobody could hear him and then almost whispering continued, "He married an Indian woman. She was very pretty and he loved her very much. She was a Flathead. When he went to set the traps one winter, she stayed at home alone. You know, the trappers always do that. He must have discovered the whole beaver town because he stayed away till the spring. When he was coming home, he knew that there was something wrong. There was no smoke coming out of the chimney and the door was open. When he walked in, he found only bones chewed up by the animals of what used to be his wife. Among her bones he saw also something that looked like a little skeleton of an unborn baby. So you can imagine how he felt. Then in the log house he found a medicine bag.

"When he looked at it there were no doubts in his mind. It was a medicine bag lost by a Crow warrior. He swore vengeance as long as he lived and any time he ran into a Crow, he killed him and ate his liver while it was still warm. They say he used to do it for many years. Yep, there are very interesting people there.

"There's old Ben. He bought a woman from a Mormon and because he had a partner who had loaned him a hundred, they used to share her, but it didn't work. Old Ben then asked his partner to pay him off and moved to Cripple Creek. Then there's the preacher who came once a month all the way from Grand Lake. He used to ride a big grey mule. When he came to Lulu City he started to preach straight from the saddle. He threatened us with eternal damnation if we don't stay away from easy women and whisky. After the sermon the mayor gave him ten dollars and he went home. On one occasion while he was painting the horrors and suffering of hell in pretty lively colors, somebody lit a dynamite stick. So you can imagine the bang. It was like firing a cannon. The mule took off, the preacher fell and everybody was laughing their heads off. Fortunately he was okay, but he had to go back by stage coach and they caught that mule all the way near Grand Lake. I am really curious if he comes again this fall. Yeah, as I said. Very interesting company."

Mike paused for a while because it occurred to him that among these "interesting people" he would have to look for a partner in order to turn his gold discovery at the Bear River into "life-long happiness," but then he just waved his hand. Not to worry, when he shows them a handful of nuggets, they will fall over each other offering their help. Maybe there will be so many he will have a hard time picking one.

The terrain changed. The area of eternal snow and bare rocks yielded to a pleasant green of coniferous growth and soft moss replacing the uneven rocky surface of the trail. The trail turned sharply to the left and followed a creek along the bottom of a deep glen. Both Mike's legs started to ache and for a moment he thought that he might sit down and rest a little, but then he rejected this idea lest he would not feel like getting up. Moreover the sun was slowly setting down and from here to Lulu City was at least another five miles. He suppressed the temptation and kept on going.

After another hour of walking the trail joined a wide road and to the left of it Mike saw a small log cabin. Great, the worst was behind him, he thought, that's Shipler's cabin. It's only another mile to town. Let's see if Shipler is at home. Mike stepped to the door, banged on it with his fist, but there was no response. Well, he is still digging or went to town to buy something. Never mind, I'll catch him later. Just a few yards from the cabin one could see the deep ruts made by a stage coach. Mike turned to the right and in spite of the pain in his leg he shuffled along the road. Don't get crazy, he admonished them. You will have plenty of opportunity to rest the whole winter, till you get tired of it. Then if you feel like going to Grand Lake, we'll take the stage coach. Suddenly, he laughed loudly and resumed his monologue aimed at Jamie.

"Yep, the stage has been running here almost for two years now, and you won't believe it, even twice a week between Grand Lake and Lulu City. At one time it had a very strange driver. We kind of thought that there was something wrong with him and sure enough it turned out it was a woman. Just a plain woman. Cross my heart. A certain Jane who drank like a man and shot like a man. It was known about her that she wasn't afraid even of a devil. Once, when she was driving this stage, a bunch of Indians got the idea that they would rob it. Now you can imagine the panic among the passengers. The ladies were screaming, the guys were turning pale, and this Jane just said—My dear Sirs, just stay calm. There has been no redskin born yet that would outsmart me and you know what she did? She grabbed the rail of the box and while holding the reins she did a handstand. She was kicking up her heels and kept yelling as if she had lost her mind. The passengers were just about to make their last wills because in addition to the trouble with the Indians their driver now went crazy and therefore they were definitely past praying for. Then they could not believe their eyes. The Indians stopped, shook their heads, turned the horses around and headed back. To cut the story short, she knew that the Indians viewed crazy people with great respect and they would never hurt them. So this trick saved her neck more than once. Some people used to say about her that she had a child and that some rich folks from the East adopted it, but you know, people gossip."

Mike suddenly interrupted his narrative about "the interesting people" of Lulu City and carefully looked at the road. Something was not right. In the evening dusk he did not notice it, but now, when the moon illuminated the landscape, he saw that there was grass growing in the stagecoach ruts. "What could it be?" he muttered. "They would run only once a week?" Then a strange uneasiness overpowered him. He began to jerk the rope and urge Jamie to walk faster. The physical pain in his old legs was now overwhelmed by a feverish anxiety. He sort of vaguely recalled comments of some miners which he overheard in the spring before his departure for the mountains. "Silver is losing its value. What they pay for an ounce wouldn't buy a handful of beans. If it keeps going like this, then I don't know..."

Mike finally spotted the dark wooden buildings of Lulu City. On the left hand side stood the stage coach station with an enclosure for horses and right across the street there was Higgins' General Store. One could buy anything there, starting with nails. Goddamn it who cares what could one buy there," Mike angrily interrupted his thoughts. "How come the light is not on? And there should be a lantern on the station." Anticipating the worst the old man's knees began to shake. Mike dropped the rope and limping with pain forced himself to run along the main street.

When he reached the Livery Stable, he began to bang on the door and call, "Pete! Pete, it's me, Mike. Open up! You can't be in bed by now! Open up!" However, grave silence was the only response. Maybe they are all at The Queen of Spades, thought Mike. He latched on to this like a drowning person to a straw. "Of course. I am an old crazy fart. Why didn't I think about it?" By sheer willpower he gathered whatever strength he had left and shuffled down the street. The Queen of Spades was in the third street on the right. When he finally made it to the saloon, he grabbed the door knob and jerking it he sharply opened the door. Instead of expected warmth and commotion of a saloon a dark, empty room stared into his face. Mike felt tears in his eyes, but he still did not want to give up. He limped back to the center of the town and in its empty streets one could hear his doleful calling, "People, where are you? Where is everybody? It's me, Mike!" and an echo, as if it were laughing at him, repeated: ike....ike...ike. After a while dead silence fell upon the abandoned town. Only in front of a hotel, which in the spring was owned by a well preserved widow of a Montana rancher, sat an old stooped man. He was looking impassively at the empty street, tears were flowing on his unshaved cheeks and he kept whispering to himself over and over, "What interesting company."

(Dedicated to the thousands of prospectors who believed
that true luck was within their reach.)

Historical Notes

Lulu City, now a ghost town, was located in Colorado in Kawuneeche Valley about 20 miles from Grand Lake. It was founded by a prospector and miner **Benjamin F. Burnett** in 1879 and named after his daughter. The area consisted of 1600 building lots. At the time when it was abandoned it had 19 streets (The First—The Nineteenth) and five avenues (Mountain, Throckmorton, Trout, Ward and Riverside). The reason for founding the town was the discovery of gold and silver along the upper part of the Grand River. At the peak of its existence the population was in the neighborhood of 500 people. Furthermore it had a post office, a general store and regular stagecoach connection to Denver through the Grand Lake. The town was abandoned about four years later partly because of the sharp drop in the value of silver and partly because of the low quality of the silver and gold ore. One of the great curiosities of the town was a large log bear trap whose remnants have been preserved till today. Currently the ghost town Lulu City is a part of the **Rocky Mountains National Park** in Colorado.

Comstock Lode was in the mountainous area near Reno, Nevada. It was rich in gold and silver ore. Henry Comstock, a trapper and prospector, discovered gold here in 1859 and a whole slew of mines which were founded shortly thereafter operated till the beginning of the 20th century.

Ophir Mine was established in the early sixties of the 19th century by the unification of numerous mining claims in the northern part of the Comstock Lode. During its operation it produced gold in value of more than eleven million dollars.

Pikes Peak and **Cripple Creek** were gold fields in Colorado, south of Denver.

Joseph L. Shipler registered his claim in 1882. The tunnel he dug in a rock wall about one hundred feet above the trail leading to Lulu City is located about a half mile from the log house where he lived. It is ironic that while Lulu City was abandoned because of low quality of silver and gold ore, two miles further west Shipler mined successfully gold for almost forty years. Eventually he built there another log house for his family. Both buildings still stand on the original site and only the roofs have collapsed.

The author also placed several popular characters of that time into this story. The coughing **Doc** is well known **John H. "Doc" Holliday,** a dentist who was a professional gambler. His fame spread because of his participation in the shootout at the O.K. Corral in **Tombstone**, Arizona. He died of tuberculosis and is buried in Glenwood Springs in Colorado.

The **"Trapper"** whose real name was **John Johnson** earned the moniker **Liver-eating Johnson** because of the incident with the Crow Indians. He served in the Union Army during the Civil War and when he died, he was buried in Los Angeles, California. In 1974 his body was exhumed and reburied in Cody, Wyoming.

The female stagecoach driver is another popular western figure, namely **Calamity Jane**, with the full name **Martha Jane Canary**. She was known in several western states, primarily due to her eccentric life. For some time she earned her living as a dance hall girl and later on she drove teams for a variety of express companies. She is buried in Deadwood, South Dakota, next to **"Wild" Bill Hickok** whom she considered to be her friend.

Old Ben and his partner are fictitious characters borrowed from the Broadway musical **"Paint Your Wagon."**

10

Frank Vejvoda

The door of a house built of square logs opened slowly and with an unpleasant creaking sound. A tall middle aged man wrapped up in warm sheepskins stepped out and began to shovel two feet of snow that had fallen during the previous night. About an hour later when the morning sun finally broke through the clouds and covered the landscape with a golden glow, one could see two dark paths in the white snow cover. One led to a large woodpile behind the house and the other one first to a well and then to a barn.

The man kept shoveling and when he made sure that the barn door could be easily opened, he pushed the shovel into a snowdrift, pulled out a handkerchief and began wiping his forehead. In the corner of his eye he caught a glimpse of smoke coming out of the chimney which meant there was breakfast being prepared at the house. The notion of a hot meal gave him extra energy.

He walked into the barn greeted by the mooing of two cows and neighing of a small brown mare, climbed up to the hayloft and then with a pitch fork he tossed hay below. Then he slowly climbed down, divided the hay among the cows and the horse. But just as he was about to leave, the rustling of straw and a strange sound resembling a human sigh caught his attention. It was coming from the stall where he used to keep the new born calves.

He stopped, carefully turned around and glanced toward the stall. In the dim light in the barn he did not see anything. It occurred to him that maybe some animal got in. But now, in January? Then he remembered that yesterday after sunset he had heard a pack of wolves howling and he shivered. No, it cannot be a wolf because the cows and the horse would go wild. At least if I had an ax here, he thought, but it's lying next to the woodpile. Then he looked at the pitchfork he had used to throw hay down. He grabbed it firmly and slowly approached the stall.

Again he heard rustling of straw and a sigh, as if someone was in pain. The man looked into the stall and froze. He ran to the barn door and jerked it open. A column of sun rays revealed the dark silhouette of a man lying on the straw, dressed in an old torn military coat and dirty deerskin pants. He wore Indian moccasins and old gloves full of holes. Blood stains were on the coat and pants. The man moved and as he turned his head into the light, the man with the pitch fork held his breath.

The uninvited guest was an Indian, and he had a long open wound that stretched from his right eye over his whole forehead, so wide that between the black edges of the skin shone the light skull bone.

The man kept staring at the Indian's bloodied head for a moment, and then pulled himself together and ran out of the barn to the house. After a couple of minutes he was back, accompanied by a stocky older boy. The man gave the boy some instructions, then grabbed the injured man under the armpits while the boy lifted his legs and they both carried him out of the barn and into the house. They carefully put him down on the wooden floor next to the fireplace, where a younger woman, the man's wife, was preparing breakfast. The whole family, including another two small children, gathered around.

The Indian must have lost lots of blood. His face was pale, his eyes were closed and his breathing was irregular. Simply said, it seemed that he would not make it until evening. The man brought a gunny sack, rolled it up and placed it under the Indian's head. Then he knelt next to him and unbuttoned his coat to see if he could find another injury, but except for that ugly wound on his head there was none. Even though he rarely got into contact with Indians he was sure that this unfortunate was a Sioux.

What was he doing here? The Sioux had their villages at least fifty miles away near the Minnesota River. At night it was at least forty below. While the man speculated about the reasons that brought this wounded man to wander to his farm, his wife warmed up a large pot of water, took a piece of linen from a large wooden trunk and started to wash off the cakes of dry blood from the Indian's face. She carefully avoided the wound which was almost five inches long and then from the same strip of fabric she fashioned a simple bandage and wrapped his forehead. The Indian did not move throughout the entire procedure and seemed to have lost consciousness. When she completed her Samaritan's work, she returned to the fireplace and continued preparing breakfast. The man in the meantime was sitting on a rough hewn bench at the table trying to think about this strange situation.

God knows if we should keep him here or not. Last fall when I took a wagon of wheat to the mill, everybody was complaining about the Indians. They sneak to a farm at night, steal a chicken or even sometimes they kill a cow, so they say. They cut it all in pieces and when a farmer wakes up, he finds only the guts lying around. They just think that there is no difference between farm animals and game. Most of the old-timers believe that the best thing to do is keep them away. There just didn't seem to be any love lost here.

I would bet a hundred dollars that if someone else found him, he would drag him out, drop him in the snow and let him freeze to death, the man thought. On the other hand, they are human beings and what kind of Christians are we if we let him die like a dog. But his thoughts were distracted by the scent of coffee and corn pancakes. There was also plenty of work waiting for him outside, so he couldn't spend the whole morning thinking about this. If that Indian makes it or not was in the Lord's hands, and then it occurred to him, let the Lord worry about whether he did a right thing or not.

After breakfast he wrapped himself in the skins and spent most of the morning hauling manure out of the barn. Shortly around noon he decided to split a bit of firewood because thanks to the Minnesota winter the pile was getting rapidly smaller and smaller. When he was about to swing the axe, he heard his wife's voice, "Get over here, quick. He just opened his eyes."

The man dropped the log and rushed inside. The Indian was not moving much but looked around the room and when he saw the man with the axe, raised his hand to a friendly greeting. Then with broken English said, "I—Black Eagle from Lower Reservation at Redwood River." Then his eyes rested on the axe and he quickly added, "Come in peace." The man suddenly realized that he was still holding the axe and he quickly leaned it against the wall and responded with no less broken English and a strong foreign accent, "Well, I Frank Vejvoda and farm here." Then he shifted from one foot to another and added, "This my wife Bozhka and children." When the Indian saw that the axe was peacefully resting at the wall and that he was not facing any imminent danger, he raised his hand toward his mouth indicating that he was hungry.

As long as he feels like eating, he is not that bad, thought Frank, but then he saw that his wife was already bringing a cup of boiled beans greased with deer tallow. The Indian could not get up, so with Frank's help he leaned up a bit on his elbows and, ignoring the spoon, quickly began to consume the food with his fingers. He must not have eaten for a quite a while, Frank thought.

When he was done, he licked his fingers, smiled gratefully and carefully touched his bandaged forehead. Frank figured that now would be the time to find out what had happened to him. However, Black Eagle, exhausted from eating slipped back on the floor, looked impassively at the ceiling and fell asleep. Only in the evening with the help of sign language and broken English did the farmer's family find out what brought Black Eagle to their farm.

There was hunger in the Indian reservations along the Redwood River. The great white father in Washington, DC promised Indians money, food and warm blankets if they surrendered their hunting grounds north of the Minnesota River to the white settlers, but all they had were his words. Food does not come regularly, money to buy provisions only rarely and the white merchants don't want to sell on credit any more. When the Indians complained at Fort Ridgely to its commander, again there was no clear answer. The great white father in the East has different worries now, he is on the great war path against the other white people in the South and he is too busy to worry about his red children in the West. The Indians have to be patient, but it is hard to be patient if there is nothing to eat.

As a result, Black Eagle and his friend Fast Wolf had a long talk and in the end they decided to leave the reservation. They would travel back to their old hunting grounds and if they succeeded in killing a deer, they would have plenty to eat. Black Eagle had an old rifle and Fast Wolf only bow and a quiver full of arrows, but Fast Wolf was a great tracker and even better shot. They walked three days, but the game was avoiding them. Finally on the fourth day they discovered a footprint of an elk. Its tracks led to a cluster of young spruces, so they split. Black Eagle went to left and Fast Wolf to the right. The Great Spirit was with them. The wind was blowing in the right direction. Fast Wolf saw the elk first. He picked up the bow and shot an arrow. Fast Wolf had not eaten for two days and his hand was weak so he only wounded the elk.

Then the Great Spirit turned away from them. The elk was a loner and it wanted to fight. Fast Wolf was a great hunter. He wanted to shoot again, but he slipped on the snow and the elk attacked him, first with his antlers and then with his front feet. Black Eagle heard his death scream and ran to help. He raised the gun and fired. He heard thunder, then he saw lightning in front of his eyes and then lost consciousness. When he woke up, he found the burst rifle and the dead body of Fast Wolf a few feet away in a pool of blood.

The elk was gone, but he could see its bloody tracks. Black Eagle followed them until he got to Blue Lake. His head hurt as if a herd of buffalos were running there, but Black Eagle knew that he must find the wounded elk, or otherwise he would die too. Before sunset he spotted a dark object in the distance. It was the dead elk with an arrow in its neck. Black Eagle cut the elk open, ate its liver, but then came a snow storm. The Great Spirit was again with him. On a hill there was a kind of building which only the white people build. That was his story.

Black Eagle spent the whole week at the Vejvoda's farm. The wound slowly began to heal and after several days he felt strong enough to go out and venture all the way to the lake. Then one day he disappeared. Frank took it in stride. He just figured Black Eagle had his reasons. Maybe he was getting bored here and longed for his own people. Maybe he will think about us sometimes.

The morning sun lazily climbed over the tree tops, burned off the fog and bright light flooded the Lower Indian Reservation located at the confluence of the Minnesota and Redwood Rivers. On an elongated plain bordered by a sharp drop on its northern side stood several structures. The prominent one was a large stone house encircled by several wooden buildings which served as warehouses for storing food, blankets and a broad variety of goods to be distributed among the local Indians. Not far away from an enclosure, where several dozens of sheep peacefully grazed, stood a small building with a patio that functioned as the reservation headquarters. To complete the picture of this western outpost of civilization one must also mention several corrals for horses, sheds for wagons and two or three piles of manure.

The place came alive shortly after sunrise. The first signs of morning activity could be detected in the warehouses that also housed several enterprising individuals who were trying to make truly unholy profits in supplying the reservation with necessary provisions.

Soon a group of men gathered on the patio in front of the house next to the sheep and surrounded a tall man with strikingly red hair. This red-haired fellow was Thomas Galbraith, the federal agent who was in charge of the Lower as well as the Upper Reservations located about thirty miles further west near the Yellow Medicine River. In the middle of August 1862 it was not an enviable job.

Galbraith was unshaven and tired. Yesterday evening five hundred armed Sioux in the Upper reservation insisted that he hand over the food regardless of the fact that the money to pay for it had not yet arrived from Washington. When he saw the frowning and resolute faces of the hungry Indians he did not resist for long and eventually produced the demanded provisions. Then he did not sleep the whole night because he knew that the Indians in the Lower Reservation would follow suit and that would probably lead to a conflict because the local merchants would refuse to open the warehouses without cash. His fears materialized even before the men on the patio could agree on a common course of action.

The area in front of the reservation headquarters suddenly filled with hundreds of Indians, who, ignoring their traditions, came with women and children. At the head of this colorful gathering stood a small man who conspicuously differed from the others by the way he dressed. Instead of clothing made out of deerskin and decorated with beads of various colors he wore dark pants, jacket with a vest and a soft black hat. Galbraith immediately recognized him as one of the chiefs, namely Little Crow. The chief raised his hand and the chattering of women and children stopped. Several warriors stepped closer and surrounded the men on the patio. Galbraith realized that the situation was getting serious and so he broke the ominous silence. With the help of the interpreter he expressed his pleasure in seeing Little Crow and then he asked the reasons behind such a large gathering of all the reservation residents. Little Crow pointed at the warehouses and then slowly as if he were weighing every word said, "Where is the money for the food? We have nothing to eat while these warehouses are full of provisions. We are asking you as a government agent to arrange the issuing of the foodstuffs or we will take them ourselves."

The Indian interpreter hesitated. He felt that he could not translate this and being at a loss as to what to say he began to stutter incoherent sentences. Galbraith then turned toward chaplain John Williamson and asked him to deliver the translation. The chaplain did exactly that and then waited for Galbraith's answer. Galbraith took this threat seriously. Just the notion as to what would happen if Little Crow carried out his threat scared the living hell out of him. He could not allow something like that to happen. He could not have it on his conscience. He slowly turned around and asked the men standing next to him their opinions. Out of several merchants who owned the warehouses only one, a certain Andrew Myrick, was present. The others were basically just paid clerks. They consulted each other and then announced with one voice that they would do what Myrick suggests.

Andrew Myrick unfortunately belonged to those merchants the Indians hated from the bottom of their hearts and he in return showed them his unbridled contempt. The Sioux had recently made the demand that Myrick must not be present when the money for the land they gave up was paid out. Before that

Myrick used to actually take large amounts under the pretext that it was the amount the Indians owed him. Quite often his and the Indians' numbers did not match and that, of course, made bad blood between them. Now Myrick had an opportunity to show the Indians who was the boss. He sharply turned away from the men around Galbraith and angrily exclaimed the fateful sentence, "Let them eat grass. What do I care!"

The Indian interpreter again refused to translate, but Little Crow did not need a translation. He knew enough English to get it. Myrick's statement caused the white men on the patio to smile, but instantly the crowd got angry. First, one could hear several exclamations that quickly changed into a hateful roar. Only the authority of Little Crow prevented the mob from attacking Galbraith and the other whites. He ordered his people to break up and return to their homes and when leaving he repeated several times just for himself, "Myrick should not have said this. No, he should not!"

Let them eat grass. Yes, the dirty, scorned Indians. Let them eat grass. What do we care? These words kept racing in the mind of the Sioux chief all the way home. So that's the way they repaid him when he had tried to be their friend, when he learned their language and their customs. That's the way they repaid him for his efforts to maintain peace and for trying to persuade his tribesmen to learn to farm just like the white people. That's what he got for his trip East where he met the great white father and assured him about his friendship. That's the way they paid him back. They threw this dirty insult in his face and kicked him away like a mangy dog. Let them eat grass. Let them die. Now we have their land, so what do we care?

In the evening Little Crow tore off the white men's clothing, dressed in the deerskin decorated with the colorful beads and put a bonnet of eagle feathers on his head. Then he walked out, turned his face toward the rising moon and raised both hands. Out of his mouth came a war cry and that night one could hear in the valley of the Minnesota and Red Rivers the low thundering sound of the tom-toms.

No, Myrick should not have said that.

Three days later, like a big red wave, the armed Sioux overran the Lower Reservation to take what belonged to them. It did not take long and the warehouses were engulfed by flames and shortly after that their burning ruins buried the mutilated bodies of the white employees who did not succeed in escaping. In front of the reservations office lay the scalped body of Myrick and in his open mouth was stuffed...grass.

Frank Vejvoda stood on a hill below his barn and with a worried look inspected the corn field. The cornstalks barely reached to his waist and that was not a good sign. By this time the corn should be up to his shoulders. It was halfway through August and they had not had a decent rain since the end of June. If we don't get a heavy rain pretty soon, the crop won't be worth much. This year is sort of lousy, thought Frank. The mare had a foal in the spring, but it was stillborn. When he was making hay in early June, it rained so much that half of it just rotted and now this drought. It is a hell of an irony. It was actually drought that drove him out of the old country across the ocean to this by-God-forgotten land.

Frank's thoughts now went back to Southern Bohemia to the region of the city of Budweiss where he was born. A year after servitude was abolished, he leased about ten acres of arable land with an old farm house and worked hard to make this field produce. His father used to laugh and kept telling him to forget farming and move to town where he could make more money. The problem was that young Frank was a farmer by heart and soul. He liked fresh air, south Bohemian ponds and lakes and the smell of freshly cut grass. He certainly did not intend to spend the whole day shut in some smelly factory. So he kept on trying, but the field that the local farmers forced for generations to produce a decent crop could not give any more.

When his first son was born, he thought about quitting and look for a job, but then fate itself intervened. It was actually his father's fault. He always wanted that farmer's almanac that the old Kreuzman sold in his bookstore in Budweiss. It was full of folk songs, folk wisdoms and weather prognoses. So one day in February Frank hitched a horse and went to Budweiss. It was the least thing he could do for his old dad. When he walked into the store, a pile of freshly printed almanacs were lying on the table right in front of him. There was picture of a saint and of a church, just like the one they have in their village, on the cover. The bookseller wanted thirty pennies, so Frank paid and because he had no reason to rush back, he opened the book and just leafed through it a little. When he was almost at the end, his eyes caught a pretty picture of a big pine forest with a lake. There were couple of big elks standing on its shore and a herd of wild geese floated in the middle of it. It was a real pleasure to look at. Right under the picture there was an inscription in Czech and German saying,

"America can be your new home." Frank thought about it for a while and then asked old Kreuzman to explain to him what it meant. Then he learned that there was an agency in Vienna that arranges emigration overseas.

The days when Frank enjoyed peace of mind were gone. He thought all the time about that picture and his barren field, and then one day after a pretty weak harvest he made an announcement at home. He was ready to pack up and go to America. Well, you get the idea what kind of an uproar it caused. Bozhka was wringing her hands and begged him not to act foolishly and that she was not going to any boonies, particularly on the other side of the world. His mother was lamenting that when she dies nobody would close her eyes and even the parish vicar called on Frank after the service and tried to persuade him to drop this idea which undoubtedly originated from the devil himself. Only his dad didn't say anything and when the women folk beseeched him to do something, he just smiled and said, "Girls, this is not so simple. Should Frankie toil from sunrise to sunset and barely make living or should he try it somewhere else? If there is really virgin land available in America, then he won't go hungry there."

Well, in the meantime spring was here again and it was time to sow. Frank bought with the last of his money several bushels of wheat and oats, he ploughed up the field, harrowed it and planted the seeds into the ungrateful soil. The last rain fell at the beginning of May and then not even a drop.

This drought was the breaking point. Frank wrote a letter to Vienna, sold his share of the house and all the farming equipment, and in the spring of the next year he and his family were embarking on a ship in Hamburg. Then in New York the agent told him that the U.S. government opened large tracts of land in Minnesota and that a bunch of Czechs had settled there already. This last piece of news made Bozhka feel a little bit better and just the thought that she would be among her countrymen helped suppress her fear of the uncertain future. However, she misjudged her Frank. When they arrived to the region settled by the Czechs, he asked, where are the lakes? Wherever he looked he saw just flat land and maybe a creek here and there, but not a decent lake. The old timers laughed and said, they didn't have any, but if he wanted to have a big pond or a lake, he would have to go further north where the Swedes and Germans were. Frank responded that he didn't mind traveling there to see the land with his own eyes. Bozhka began to cry that she was not going to live among these foreigners, but Frank didn't give in. For almost two years he carried in his mind the picture of that lake with elks and wild geese he had seen in the almanac. He survived the trip across the ocean and traveled over half of the American continent to give up his dream just before it was in his reach? He left his wife and the boy with a Czech family and ventured north by himself.

When he arrived at Blue Lake, he saw his dream come true. The lake was partly surrounded by a dense forest of pine and oak trees and near the shore in the reeds he could hear the wild geese and ducks and God knows what kind of other water fowl. Then in the evening herds of elk and deer came to drink the crystal clear water from the lake. Moreover, on the eastern side of the lake he saw an open slope just waiting for a plough to turn the rich Minnesota soil.

As Frank was admiring the lake whose blue surface reflected several white clouds, he spotted a wagon pulled by a pair of oxen on the road. The driver was his neighbor, Mr. Hoffman, a German. He was probably returning from the mill, Frank thought. He was doing really well. He had come about a year after Frank, but had two big boys and so he had his house and the barn up in no time with less drudgery. It looks like he was in a rush or he would have stopped for a chat. Well, it was time for lunch.

Frank turned around and slowly walked toward the house. Suddenly, he saw the silhouette of man running behind the barn. Well, we aren't expecting anybody, he thought and walked faster. Then the stillness was interrupted by a woman's piercing scream. Frank looked toward the house and what he saw made his blood curdle. Two painted Indians were dragging Bozka and his children out of the house. What the hell are these savages doing? Don't they have enough of their own women? In a few leaps he reached the wagon near the shed, grabbed the swingle tree, but two Indians who were hiding behind the barn jumped him. Frank fought like a devil, but he did not have a chance against experienced fighters like the Sioux. They knocked him down, tied him up with a rope and then one of them raised his hand holding a tomahawk. Frank closed his eyes and tried not think about the heart-breaking screams of his wife.

The death blow, however, did not come. Another Indian appeared on the scene and yelled something in his native tongue. The hand with the tomahawk stopped in midair and the two Indians stepped aside. Frank slowly got up. An Indian covered with war paint in his face and on his chest sat on a horse several feet from him. The thick layer of the vermillion, however, could not completely cover the deep scar stretched from his right eye over his forehead. On a brown and white paint sat Black Eagle.

The stillness of the forest was interrupted only by the snapping of twigs under the iron tires of a small farm wagon. A brown horse was pulling against a leather collar and from time to time it shook its head to get rid of the bothersome flies. A man in a broad hat like the one the local farmers wore walked silently along the wagon and drove the horse. Two children surrounded by several wooden trunks, featherbeds and miscellaneous household items sat on the wagon. Two cows were urged to walk faster by a younger woman and an older boy followed right behind.

Finally as a rearguard, an Indian, his face and chest covered with war paint, rode on a spotted horse. The faces of all members of this family reflected fatigue and exhaustion and the face of the young woman and the children bore tear marks.

The Indian suddenly urged his horse, caught up with the man walking along the wagon and with a hand gesture asked him to stop. Then he dismounted and with broken English began to explain something. The man nodded his head that he understood and then stretched out his hand. The Indian shook it firmly, jumped into a primitive saddle covered with a buffalo skin, and headed back along the ruts made by the wagon.

The husband and wife, whose worldly possessions consisted of two cows and the wagon loaded with personal items, began to talk. As they did not speak either Swedish or German, but rather in an unusually soft sounding language, the reader could easily figure out that they were none else than Frank, Bozhka, and their children who stood here alone in the middle of the Minnesota wilderness considering their next steps. After a while, Frank clicked his tongue and the horse leaned against the collar. About a half an hour later the forest thinned out and they walked on the open prairie.

Black Eagle did not lie.

H'm, Black Eagle, thought Frank. If it were not for him, I would be pushing up daisies by now, or as the Indians say I would be in the eternal hunting grounds. He showed up really five minutes to twelve and for that I am grateful, but the news he brought was straight from hell. He said that the Indians in the Lower Reservation had risen up, broken out and slaughtered the white farmers left and right. If we want to save our necks the only way is to go to Fort Ridgely. Little Crow is calling up the warriors from the reservations which means that it will take two or three days before he goes on the war path. If we can make it to the fort, we'll be okay. It is well built and there is no chance he could take it.

The Vejvodas came to a small stream, just a brook hemmed by willow trees on both sides. Following Black Eagle's instructions, Frank turned the wagon to the right and stayed on the right bank. The stream should take them all the way to Fort Ridgely. Everybody felt a little bit better. They had been traveling since yesterday and thanks only to their Indian guide had they made it without any trouble and did not get lost in the forest. Yesterday in the evening they camped in the middle of a clearing, but to be on the safe side they did not make fire. The excitement and worries about what the next day would bring did not allow either Frank or Bozhka to sleep. They just restlessly rolled under the blankets and Frank kept making sure that his shotgun was within reach. Only the children slept like logs. At the crack of dawn Bozhka milked one cow, Frank hitched the horse and before the sun cleared the horizon, they were again on the way.

The landscape did not change much. Occasionally a little hill appeared on the monotonous plain or the creek decided to add to its straight bed several bends. The afternoon sun was burning the dry land and the suffering of our pilgrims caused by the unbearable heat was worsened by clouds of mosquitoes and horseflies. Frank walked with his head down preoccupied with his own thoughts which eventually turned into a sort of dialogue between two mutually disagreeing voices:

What made them rampage like this? Who ever saw it to kill innocent people without any reason?

What do you mean without a reason? You don't remember that Black Eagle complained that there was nothing to eat on the reservation?

So why didn't they hunt before the winter? They should think ahead of time. They knew that winter was coming.

And where are they supposed to hunt if people like you took their land?

I didn't take anything from anybody. I've got papers for that land at the lake from the government.

And where do you think, you wise guy, the government got that land?

Okay, but there is plenty of land here. Why don't they learn to farm like us? Then neither of us would go hungry.

Look, they lived for generations their own ways and it worked for them, so why should they live differently now? Would you like to move into a teepee and learn to kill buffalos by bow and arrow because some weird people overran your country? Hardly, eh.

Frank realized that he would not be able to solve this argument any time soon and so by waving his hand he chased both voices away and paid attention to the landscape they were passing through. Suddenly, he noticed that the horse quickened his pace as if he smelled horse manure and connected it to an image of a stable and a bucket of oats. Frank looked around and sure enough he noticed a small dwelling built out of logs and sods with an enclosure for cattle on a small rise. He urged the horse and after a while he stopped, told Bozhka to water the horse by the stream and by himself he walked along a narrow beaten trail to the house.

The place was quiet, and only a light wind rustled the short cornstalks. Well, his corn does not look any better than mine, thought Frank and banged on the door which was partially open. No one responded, so he called, "Anybody home?" No answer. Frank opened the door and entered. He looked around the room and instantly froze, horrified.

A farmer sat at the table and in his open, blood-stained shirt stuck two arrows. His hands were hanging limply along his torso, the head was pushed back and his dead eyes stared at the ceiling. Instead of hair there was large wound on top of his skull covered by flies. In his open mouth he could see food the dead man did not have time to swallow. Death obviously caught this unfortunate farmer during his lunch.

Frank then glanced into the corner. His knees began to shake and he felt nauseated. On a primitive bed lay a naked woman with her head split by an axe and scalped, just like the man at the table. Then Frank began to throw up. The woman's belly was cut open and next to it was a bloody bundle, an unborn child. Frank closed his eyes, wiped his mouth and once the racking feeling subsided, turned around, and by sheer willpower forced his legs to carry him out into the open.

Then he closed the door and slowly as if he were in a dream, walked down to the wagon where his family was waiting for him. He did not answer Bozhka's question about what he had found out, only grabbed the reins and using the whip urged to horse forward. When Bozhka asked why they were moving on, Frank turned his face away from her and stiffly blurted out, "They were not at home." Then he cracked the whip and kept looking around to see if he could see anything that would betray the presence of those who perpetrated this horrible crime, but there was no sign of any human being far and wide.

Bozhka felt that something was not right, but she did not press any more questions. Frank kept on walking in long strides next to the horse and tried to guess how many more miles they had to go before they reached safe haven. The children, tired by the afternoon heat, slumbered on the wagon and the horse steadily plodded through the high grass. The terrain was flat and open so there was no need to stop and rest too often.

Then suddenly a dark dot appeared in the distance. Frank turned around and called to Bozhka, "I think we have made it!"

Shortly after sunset the half fagged out and lathered horse staggered onto the parade grounds of Fort Ridgely.

The exhausted Vejvodas were met by a group of scared to death refugees who arrived at the fort a day earlier. Many were barefooted, their clothing was torn and some of them wore only nightshirts. There were no doubts that they had fled in fearful panic to save their bare skins. Some were warned by friendly Indians, and the others were not at home through some act of Providence when the slaughter started and so they escaped sure death. Frank and Bozhka listened to the complaints about the Sioux atrocities until late at night and then it occurred to them that they had survived this human tragedy because of Black Eagle.

They spent the night in a small shack next to the stone building that housed the soldiers. Frank slept like a man who walked almost thirty miles. Only toward morning he dreamed about Bozhka who was tied up and carried away by a horde of Indians. He tried to run to help her, but his legs were like lead, and he could hardly move. She kept screaming louder and louder and then...he woke up. No, it was not Bozhka, she slept quietly next to him. The noise was the yelling of several hundred warriors who under the leadership of the Little Crow decided to attack the fort at sunrise.

Frank got up and woke up Bozhka and the children. By now the Indians had fired several shots at the fort and up to four hundred warriors began to run toward its walls. Then a salvo from numerous rifles cracked from the ramparts followed by the low thunder of cannon fire. The Sioux hit the ground and hidden in the tall grass they tried to get closer and pour lead as well as arrows at the defending garrison. The soldiers in the blue uniforms managed to stop the first and second wave and when by noon the ranks of the attacking warriors got significantly thinner, Little Crow ordered a retreat.

Lieutenant Sheehan who directed the defense walked around the fortification to get reports about the casualties among his men and then walked down to the parade grounds. There he ordered all the men to line up who had sought refuge at the fort and turned to them with the following request, "I need any man who knows how to shoot. In case the savages get reinforced and attack again, I'll need men on the ramparts. Anybody who wants to volunteer, raise your hand!"

For a while it was quiet, but then one man after the other raised his hand. When it was Frank's turn he responded like most of the other farmers. Bozhka ran to him and begged him to reconsider, to think about her and the children, but Frank just turned his head and with quiet but firm voice said, "Bozhka, you have no idea what would happen to us if the Indians got hold of this fort."

Lieutenant Sheehan then handed out Springfield rifles to all the volunteers, made sure they knew how to load them and finally every man received a powder flask and a dozen bullets. The area around the fort was quiet for almost two hours. Most of the soldiers believed Little Crow decided that it was safer to attack the farmers' homesteads than a fort defended by a disciplined garrison and that he pulled back to the reservation.

But, suddenly, the afternoon calm was broken by the war hoops of Indian warriors who with the strength of about eight hundred men tried again to breach the fort defenses. Little Crow had gotten reinforcements.

Frank and the other volunteers immediately took their places on the ramparts as some two hundred horsemen colorfully painted and on richly decorated mounts rode in full gallop toward them in a spread-out line. At the same moment they heard the lieutenant's voice telling them not to shoot before he gives an order. Frank realized that he never killed anybody. A couple of times as a young strapping youth he got into a fight over a girl, but that was all. Except for some bruises nobody got seriously hurt. Now he is supposed to...

His thoughts were interrupted by a sharp command: "Aim!" Frank felt a strange calm, all nervousness gone. In his mind he saw the murdered farmer and his wife and then he thought about his farm at the lake that he had to leave after ten years of toiling and deprivation. Frank carefully aimed into the red wave of approaching Indians and the moment he heard the command "Fire!" he pulled the trigger.

Little Crow was determined to take the fort this time. He kept sending one wave of warriors against its defenders after another, but to no avail. At one time the Indians succeeded in breaking on to the parade grounds through lightly defended stables, but Sergeant Jones, an old veteran who commanded a battery of Howitzers, turned one of the cannons around, loaded it with broken horse shoes, nails and any pieces of metal he could find and fired at the intruders from close range. After the second shot the Indians cleared out of the fort and toward the evening with a loss of almost four hundred men they retreated toward the Lower Reservation.

A couple of days later Colonel Sibley arrived at the fort with one thousand five hundred men, mostly experienced Indian fighters and woodsmen. Against such a force Little Crow had no chance.

The Vejvodas remained at the fort till mid-November. They lived on the modest supplies they had managed to bring with them and they sold one cow. When Colonel Sibley announced that Little Crow had retreated to the Dakota Territory and that he planned to spend the winter in Canada, Frank decided it was time to go home. The word spread that the other Indians were in prison camps and that those Sioux who committed massacres of individual farmers would be tried and punished. The officers asked that if someone could provide testimony in someone's favor or disfavor, he should report it to an appropriate authority. Frank did not wait for long and truthfully narrated the whole story about Black Eagle to the fort commander and he did not forget to emphasize that only thanks to him he and his family were alive. He also mentioned the murdered farmer and his wife they saw along the way to the fort. The commander kept nodding his head, wrote everything down and then assured Frank that the courts would make sure that justice would be done. The Vejvodas then packed their personal effects, Frank hitched the same horse with which they had come and with one cow tied up behind the wagon they headed back to Blue Lake.

The house and the barn were untouched. It seemed that no human being had passed through their homestead at all while they were gone. Agricultural equipment, furnishings in the house and simply everything was in its place just like they had left it.

Soon the horse and cow were in their old barn and Frank threw them some hay. Then he walked to the lake to look at his cornfield. It was not a cheerful sight. Here and there one could see a little corn ear with a handful of yellow seeds but most of the cornstalks were broken and dozens of small and large hoof prints confirmed Frank's prediction that whatever corn had ripened was eaten by deer and elks. Well, Frank reasoned, one can always plant new corn but one cannot put a new head on one's neck. In the spring I'll borrow pair of oxen from Hoffman and start from scratch.

Suddenly, a startled feeling ran through his body. Hoffmann...Jesus Christ, what if he met the same fate as that farmer along the creek? He had wanted to go and warn him, but Black Eagle had frowned and said there was no time for it. All that time Frank didn't feel good about it, but he kept consoling himself that maybe Hoffmann would be lucky and the Indians would miss his place.

The next morning he set out to see. The Hoffmanns' farm stood on the other side of the lake in a valley. He left his loaded shotgun at home and told Bozhka to bar the door and not let anybody in until he got back. He put the Springfield rifle he had brought home from the fort on his shoulder and headed out. The ground was covered with only a slight snow dusting, but the reeds in the lake were locked in a sheet of ice. Then it occurred to him that several months ago he would not have been able to hurt another human being, but now he would speed a bullet though the head of any hostile Indian who would cross his path. After walking for about an hour he spotted in the rising fog the house and then the barn of Hoffmann's place.

Right away he saw that something was amiss. No smoke coming out of the chimney, the garden and the cattle enclosure were overgrown with weeds and the little pen where one could always hear pigs grunting was quiet. Frank walked around the barn, then slowly approached the house looking for any signs of life, but he saw nothing. Suddenly, he noticed a pile of freshly split wood. Someone must be here. He headed directly to the door when a window shutter about two inches thick opened slightly and Frank saw a black gun barrel pointed at him. It scared him so much that he almost dropped his muzzleloader, but he called out, "Don't shoot! It's me, Frank!"

The gun barrel disappeared, the heavy oak door opened and a stooped man with a long white beard stepped onto the threshold. With sunken eyes he looked Frank over and quietly, with a strong German accent said, "Come in."

Frank could not believe his eyes. This is my neighbor Hoffmann? When he had last seen him, sometime in the summer, he was a hell of a big man and even though he was over fifty, he didn't have a single white hair. Now, he was a shadow of what he used to be and when he took off his hat, his hair was snow white. Frank slowly sat down at the table as Hoffman indicated, didn't say anything for a while and then quietly asked about his family. Hoffmann got up, opened the window shutter on the other side of the room and then, and without saying a word pointed toward the woods. There, a large mound overgrown with fall grass looming black under a tall spruce were three crosses. Frank dropped his head, muttered something like an expression of sympathy. Then he quietly asked, "Indians?" The white-haired man nodded.

Hoffmann moved over to the fireplace, lit the kindling and half in German and half in English described what had happened. When Hoffmann returned from the mill, his two sons and wife were dead. He found the sons not far from the barn covered with arrows and his wife was in the house lying on the floor next to the fireplace with her head split. He thought he would go mad with anguish. He ran around the house and cursed God for such a horrible and unjust fate. He calmed down toward evening, carried the mutilated bodies of both sons into the house and barricaded the door. Then he waited to see if the Indians would come back. In the morning he buried the bodies and then went to Frank's place. He carefully searched the house and the barn, but came to the conclusion that someone must have warned the Vejvodas and they managed to escape this horror. When he returned home, he decided to stay. If he was to die, at least it would be next to his loved ones. Since that time he had never seen another living soul.

Frank began slowly to understand why Black Eagle had insisted that they leave right away and why he didn't want him to warn the Hoffmanns. Who then committed that awful atrocity? Black Eagle's people or someone else?

Frank stayed with Hoffman for a while, offered any help he might need and sadly took his leave. He would probably never find out how Hoffman's life had been destroyed.

Back on his farm, Frank began to worry how they were going to make it through the winter because they had not brought enough provisions from Fort Ridgely. He kept wracking his brain with the thought that death and destruction rained everywhere around them and he and his family were the only people who had come out of it unscathed. Frank was not a religious person, but he kept asking himself questions that he hadn't had much time to consider before. He wondered if it was only an accident that an unknown wounded Indian wandered to his place and that the same Indian came six months later to save their lives. Or was it Providence that guided his steps? Then he decided that he could not forget about it just like that. If it had been in the old country, he would have had a small shrine built like that farmer whose team of horses ran away. When he thought that he was past praying for, he believed that the Virgin Mary appeared and stopped the horses. It was a beautiful shrine right in the middle of the village, but who would consecrate such a shrine here? There is no Catholic priest for a hundred miles around because most of the local farmers are Germans or Swedes and they are either Lutherans or Calvinists. Then he got an idea that would solve this problem. I'll build a large cross at the lake so anybody could see from afar that this is not an ordinary place and with no Catholic church in the area, we'll go there every Sunday and pray at this cross so the Lord will not think that the Vejvodas don't know what gratitude is.

Sometime in the middle of December Frank went into the woods and cut down a tall fir to implement his plan. Then, with his horse he dragged it to the house and began to build a large cross. At the same time, about seventy miles south at Fort Mankato in the frosty morning the guards were leading a large group of Indians shackled in chains toward a big scaffold. The Indians then slowly stepped upon the place of execution and the military hangman placed a hemp noose around their necks.

The Indians began to sing. Some sang Indian songs of death, the others psalms they had learned from the white missionaries. As the hangman was placing the noose on the last convict, he noticed a long scar that stretched from his right eye over his whole forehead. He just shook his head, stepped down from the scaffold and at given command pulled a wooden lever.

The trapdoor opened and the singing stopped.

(Dedicated to the memory of the Minnesota settlers who died during the Sioux uprising in 1862.)

Historical Notes

The characters in this story are mostly fictitious except for the federal agent Thomas J. Galbraith, Andrew Myrick, Lieutenant Timothy J. Sheehan, Colonel Henry H. Sibley and the Indian Chief Little Crow. The historical background for the story consists of two components, on one hand the actual Sioux uprising and on the other the events tied to the Indian wife of **Joseph R. Brown,** the federal agent who was in charge of both reservations between the years 1857–1861. During the day when the warehouses of the white merchants were destroyed he was away from the reservation getting ready for his trip to New York. Friends of the family warned his wife about the potential danger and she decided to flee with ten children and two grandchildren to Fort Ridgely. However, along the way they were intercepted by a group of Indians led by the infamous chief **Shakopee**. Only the presence of a young Indian warrior, whom Mrs. Brown had rescued from freezing to death the previous winter, saved her from certain death. Mrs. Brown and the children were taken captive and kept in an Indian camp under the direct oversight of **Little Crow**. Due to the pressure of the advancing troops led by **Colonel Henry H. Sibley,** Little Crow retreated to the Dakota Territory and all prisoners were eventually released.

A few words about the actual uprising. The revolt was triggered by the murder of the entire family of **Postmaster Robinson Jones** near Ackton by four Indian youngsters who wanted to prove to themselves that they were not cowards. When they returned to their village on Rice Creek they announced that they had started the war against the white people. Considering the disastrous conditions in both reservations most of the chiefs expressed support for war whose purpose was to drive the white settlers permanently out of their original hunting grounds. Little Crow, the local war chief, however vehemently opposed any attempt to provoke an armed conflict since he was fully familiar with the military might of the U.S. government in spite of the ongoing Civil War. Only when accused of being a coward, the most serious accusation in the Indian culture, he grudgingly agreed. His warriors suffered three major defeats. One at Fort Ridgely, then at a place called **Birch Coulee** and finally near the **Yellow Medicine River**. They succeeded only in destruction of the town of **New Ulm**.

After the occupation of the Indian camp at the Yellow Medicine River Colonel Sibley ordered the arrest of up to 600 warriors and tried them by the military courts. At the end of the trials (November 5th, 1862) 303 of them were found guilty of atrocities against the local population, namely the killing of approximately 800 people. Considering such a high number of prisoners condemned to death Colonel Sibley decided to ask the White House to make the final decision. President Abraham Lincoln forwarded the files to two lawyers who carefully went through all individual cases and came to the conclusion that only thirty-nine warriors were found guilty beyond any doubt. The execution was carried out on December 26th, 1862 at Fort Mankato. The rest of the Santees (one of the three major tribes of the Sioux nation living originally in today's Minnesota), approximately 1700 people, were shipped by boats on the Minnesota River to the **Crow Creek Reservation** in Dakota.

What happened to the three major chiefs—**Shakopee, Medicine Bottle** and **Little Crow**? They all escaped to Canada. Shakopee and Medicine Bottle were staying at **Fort Garry** while the whereabouts of Little Crow were not clear. He was allegedly trying to convince the Canadian officials to provide military help in his struggle with Colonel Sibley, but the Canadians were not interested in provoking a diplomatic conflict with the U.S. and refused. They only offered Little Crow and his band some food, but no weapons. In the meantime **Major Edwin Hatch** pulled off the spectacular kidnapping of Shakopee and Medicine Bottle with the help of one American and two Canadian citizens. Both chiefs were drugged, then tied up, loaded on sleighs pulled by dogs and transported to the American side to the town of **Pembina**. Then they were handed over to Colonel Sibley, tried by a military court, found guilty and executed.

Little Crow, after failing to secure Canadian assistance, decided to return to the U.S. and join the other Sioux, namely the Lakota, to secure food by hunting buffalos like the other prairie Indians. However, for that he needed horses and those could be obtained from the Minnesota farmers. By the beginning of July in 1863 Little Crow and a group of sixteen warriors camped near the town of **Hutchinson**. One afternoon Little Crow and his son **Wowinapa** were picking berries when they ran into two white settlers—**Nathan Lampson** and his son **Chauncey** who were returning from a hunt. Considering the previous events and a reward of $25 for the scalp of a dead Santee, they immediately opened fire. Wowinapa escaped, but Little Crow fell mortally wounded. The settlers then brought the chief's dead body to Hutchinson in order to warn the rest of the farmers about the potential danger of some Indians still roaming in the area.

Several days later Wowinapa was caught and promptly condemned to death, but the court in Washington, DC considered his age and changed the verdict to jail time. (After his release Wowinapa changed his name to **Thomas Wakeman**, became a preacher and later on founded among the Sioux the popular organization YMCA.) When Colonel Sibley heard about the incident, he traveled to Hutchinson to see the dead body. If it was true that the boy's father was Little Crow, the right hand would have the deformed right wrist, a reminder of an injury Little Crow suffered from an enemy rifle. After his arrival in Hutchinson, Sibley ordered the corpse to be dug up from the town dump, and sure enough, the right wrist was crooked. It was the dead body of Tha-oya-te-duta—Little Crow.

11
Joseph L. Haywood

(Based on True Events)

Life in town bore the effects of the mid-day oppressive heat. Everything was silent. The rattling of buggies that moved up and down the main street and the town square during the morning were not heard as often. Carpenters found a comfortable spot in the shade of the nearby trees or unfinished buildings and small groups of people who normally filled the sidewalks had practically disappeared.

Some folks found refuge from the heat in the local stores, others in the lobby of the recently finished hotel Dampier. A horse covered with sweat and hitched to a green cart with the sign US Mail walked slowly along the main street, occasionally swishing its tail to get rid of pesky flies. At each stop it patiently waited for a short fellow in a broad trimmed hat until he delivered a handful of letters or a little parcel and then slowly continued its journey through the sweltering town. Northfield, just like many other settlements on the Midwestern plains, suffered the last quirks of the hot summer. Even though, according to the calendar, it was the beginning of September, the thermometer behaved as if it was the middle of July.

Several local matrons argued about something in front of a two story corner edifice built out of grey sandstone, but these ladies disappeared after a while into the store located inside. A black and white sign simply announced that its proprietors were Lee and Hitchcock and that the nature of this establishment was a general store. On the other side of the building facing the main street stood a small hitching post in front of a tall glass door. The hitching post threw a narrow strip of shade where two panting dogs seemed to have found protection from the burning sun. A quite oversized sign over the glass door made all passersby aware that Northfield also had a branch of The First National Bank.

Inside the bank, in an elongated room whose stone walls provided a cool place, sat two men near a massive oak counter worrying about columns of numbers rather than the heat that tortured the town. One man about forty years old with a thick black beard sat with his back toward a door leading to the room with a large safe. He was working on a report about the last month's deposits. This man was Joseph L. Haywood, the treasurer, a man responsible for all the money the local people had entrusted into the care of this bank. The other man, a bit younger and also with a beard that was flowing all the way to his chest, was Frank J. Wilcox, the bookkeeper who was in charge not only of all financial transactions, but was also supposed to see that the bank made a profit and that the loans provided to the customers were covered with proper collaterals. Wilcox sat at a small writing desk and tried to reconcile the columns of debits and credits. Unfortunately, there was an extra two hundred dollars in the debit column and even though he had been racking his brain with this problem since the morning, he was not close to any satisfactory solution.

The silence interrupted only by rustling of paper was suddenly broken by the sound of a striking clock which announced that it was high noon. At the same time Haywood heard a faint and hardly noticeable click. He smiled and thought that after all that effort a miracle eventually happened—he had succeeded to harmonize the time lock in the safe with the pendulum clock on the wall. Haywood got up, grabbed a small metal box which contained cash deposits received this morning and entered the room behind him. Then he stepped up to a large steel safe painted black and green with a small brass plaque saying "Evans and Watson, Philadelphia, Pa." Haywood ran his fingers over the complex mechanism of the lock, turned it into the correct position and opened the safe. Stacks of bank notes and coins which had accumulated during the last two weeks and whose value could be estimated at about ten thousand dollars rested on black shelves waiting for a safe transportation to St. Paul. Haywood emptied the metal box, placed paper money and coins on appropriate piles and closed the steel door. He was just about to reset the lock, when something occurred to him. He turned around and walked out of the room and sat down at the counter.

As he bent over the ledger, horses' hooves thundered on the wooden bridge at the lower part of the square and in the hot quivering air one could see eight riders. They wore dark hats and even though the mercury reached ninety degrees, all men wore not only long dusters, but for some reason they were buttoned up all the way to their necks. They rode long legged horses whose light and quick gait was typical of the thoroughbreds from the East, maybe even from Kentucky. The saddles as well as the bridles and bits indicated that the owners of these magnificent animals had not spared money and bought only the best. At any rate, these riders made the impression that they belonged to a class of well off people, probably cattlemen or real estate speculators or just a group of city slickers from St. Paul who came to Northfield to do some hunting.

On the other side of the bridge the group split up. Three riders headed across the square directly to the main street and the rest of them turned to the right and followed the river bank. They then turned to the left and disappeared in the first street behind the square.

Haywood's finger kept sliding up and down a column of numbers and names of customers who patronized the bank and then it suddenly stopped at a strange name. Haywood raised his head and with voice full of excitement turned toward Wilcox who was doggedly trying to find out where those two hundred dollars came from.

"Mr. Wilcox, this is amazing. There are customers coming here all the way from New Prague which is at least half a day's trip. Please, have a look, here." And saying that he pushed the ledger under Wilcox's nose. Wilcox was definitely not in the mood to interrupt his search for the origin of the extra amount because of an out of town customer with an exotic name, but being polite he raised his head and gave the thick leather bound book a quick look. Then Haywood further inquired whether he had ever been in New Prague. Wilcox shook his head and was about to bury it again in the papers but Haywood sensed serious gaps in the knowledge of local geography on the part of his colleague, and began to fill them in.

About that time the three riders in the long dusters reached the upper section of the square, stopped and carefully looked around the main street. The green mail cart was long gone and except for two or three pedestrians the town did not show any signs of life. The men headed their horses toward the hitching post in front of the bank.

"You simply have to see it, Mr. Wilcox," Haywood with poorly hidden excitement continued. "I was there with my wife last year, and as luck would have it, they had some sort of a fair. It had a strange name, let me think, yeah, I remember, they called it something like dozhinkee. Streets were crowded with people, and you would not believe how smartly they were dressed. Girls and young women wore colorfully embroidered skirts with laced slips, and the shirts, by God, the shirts. They had large pleated and starched sleeves. Simply amazing! Then they put together a band and played beautiful songs. Of course we couldn't understand a word. Some sounded a little melancholy, but others were pretty joyful. Then we stopped at stands loaded with their native food, and I have to admit, it was really tasty stuff."

The moment Wilcox caught the word food, he became attentive. He put the pen aside and asked what specific foods he was talking about. Haywood readily obliged and started describing a variety of cookies, pastries and other sweet stuffs the wives of the Czech farmers baked and did not forget about the strange sausages stuffed into hog intestines and secured at each end with something like a toothpick. Then he thought for a moment and added, "I think they call it a liver sausage."

Wilcox, definitely showing interest, nodded his head and Haywood continued his monologue. "Although we didn't understand them much, you know some spoke only broken English, I had some sort of a feeling that these were jovial people, or how should I say it, they simply made a good impression. And they are hardworking people and quite skillful. Actually I would venture to say that one could learn a lot from them. On the way home we both agreed that we should visit them again. Actually, what do you think, since you have never been there, that we rent a carriage and go there this fall together. I am sure your missus would like it there too."

Wilcox pretended that he was giving this idea a serious thought and after a while when Haywood returned to the culinary skills of the Czech settlers, he finally gave in. The notion of a carriage ride when all the maples, elms, oaks and cottonwoods glow with a multitude of colors and a pair of horses will carry them to a nice outing broke up, at least for while, the official atmosphere that filled the grey bank room and it was filled with pleasant ambiance.

Meanwhile, the three men dismounted in front of the bank, chased the dogs away and tied up their horses to the hitching post. On the other side of the building the other five rode slowly in the direction of the bank.

Haywood was about to say that he knew a fellow who goes to New Prague on a regular basis and he could find out the exact date of this year's fair, when suddenly one could hear clinks of spurs on the sidewalk. Then the door opened and three men walked in. One of them, a younger guy with strikingly blue eyes, stepped up to the counter, pulled out of his pocket a fifty dollar bill and asked

Haywood, if he could break it. Haywood nodded and took the banknote. The stranger asked another question. "Are you the treasurer?"

"Yes, Sir," was the answer. Haywood reached for the change and then he could not believe his ears. "Well, that's good, so you can open the safe for us," the blue eyed fellow coolly remarked. For a second Haywood thought it had to be a joke, but when he stared at the dark barrel of a revolver, he realized the full meaning of those words. No, it was not a joke, it was an armed robbery.

Events then took a rather dramatic turn. The other two men—one a younger handsome fellow with a mustache and the other one a tall guy with a loutish facial expression—jumped over the counter and with guns in their hands forced Wilcox to get up and stand with his raised hands next to the wall. Haywood in the meantime recovered from the initial shock and rushed to the open door leading to the room with the safe to slam it shut. But the blue eyed fellow was faster, put his foot in the door, buried the barrel of his gun into Haywood's ribs and hissed in a low voice, "No foolish stuff! Get in and open the damned safe!"

These guys are professionals and this is not their first robbery, thought Haywood. Nevertheless he remained calm and readily answered that it was not possible because the safe had a time lock and he did not remember the combination. It seemed for a second that his response surprised them, but really only for a second. The barrel of the gun moved to his temple and the same voice ordered, "So try to remember!" Haywood feverishly thought what to do. The instinct of self-preservation was telling him to comply, but at the same time he recollected the emphatic words of the bank president that he as treasurer was responsible for all the money in the safe and that he had to guard it like his own because in case of a robbery or some other kind of loss nobody will replace the savings of the town's people and the local farmers. Haywood decided to take a chance, "I am really sorry, but I cannot open it."

When the other tall bandit who was in the meantime rummaging in the drawers heard it, he turned around and with a curse, "I'll teach that son of a bitch," leapt toward the treasurer and with the butt of his revolver hit him over the head. Haywood fell on his knees. Then the robber pulled out a knife and put it on his neck. The sharp pain in his head prevented Haywood from clear thinking. Suddenly he felt on his neck and chest a strange warmth. The knife must have cut the vein. Like in a dream he heard a coarse voice ordering him to open the safe. Out of his mouth came only a desperate call for help. Then a shot cracked outside and instantly another followed. One of the bandits who was watching outside tore the door open and yelled at the men inside, "Let's get out of here. They opened fire on us!"

The situation in the bank changed dramatically. The bandit with the knife pushed Haywood aside, jumped over the counter and ran to the door. The good looking guy with the mustache joined him and the blue eyed fellow sailed over the counter right behind him. However, he stopped at the door, turned around and looked at the bloodied Haywood who had pressed one hand to his neck and was leaning with the other on the floor as he tried to get up. Then he calmly aimed his revolver at Haywood's forehead and a shot thundered in the grey room.

In the meantime, the area in front of the bank became the scene of a wild gun battle. Reports of rifles and revolvers mixed with the loud screaming of wounded horses filled the main street. Then the shooting stopped just as suddenly as it started. One could only hear the disappearing pounding of hooves and then excited voices. Shortly after that the bank door opened and the sheriff, accompanied by two other men, walked in. They slowly passed the counter and spotted Wilcox who was scared to death but otherwise okay.

The sheriff carefully stepped over Haywood's body, avoided the growing pool of blood and entered the back room. Then he stepped up to the safe and just out of curiosity pulled the door handle. He could hardly hide his surprise when the door opened and there on the black shelves he saw stacks of banknotes and coins waiting for safe transportation to the central bank in St. Paul.

Historical Notes

The failed attempt to rob the Northfield bank on September 7, 1876 basically ended the infamous existence of two gangs led by the **James** brothers (**Jesse and Frank**) and **Younger** brothers (**Cole, Jim and Bob**). Thanks to the bravery of the local citizens, namely **Henry W. Wheeler, Anselm R. Manning** and **Elias Stacy** the bandits were forced to flee town without getting the money from the bank and moreover two of them (**Clel Miller** and **Bill Chadwell**) lay dead in the dust of the main street. Bleeding from several wounds the bandits fled in the southwest direction, but after two weeks of an intensive manhunt they were caught by a posse led by Sheriff **James Glispin**. After a short but desperate resistance near the community of **Madelia** in which one of the bandits **Charlie Pitts** was killed the rest of the band surrendered. Jesse and his brother Frank, however, were not among them.

They separated from the Younger brothers shortly after the flight from Northfield and reached the Dakota Territory where they remained in hiding for a long period of time. Any further information about their activity is rather sketchy. On April 3, 1882 the newspaper in St. Joseph (Missouri) brought sensational news. Jesse James was shot by **Bob Ford**, a member of a newly formed gang to collect the reward of $5000. Frank James, who knew that the Pinkerton detectives were on his heels, surrendered to the Missouri authorities on September 5th of the same year. Frank was tried but since the witnesses consisted primarily of southern sympathizers including a former general of the Confederate army and testified in Frank's favor, he was found not guilty. Frank James died in bed at the age of 75 years.

Except for Joseph L. Haywood the loss of life among the Northfield citizens during the robbery were minimal. Some were lightly wounded, such as the third bank clerk **Alonzo E. Bunker** who managed to escape which is why he is not mentioned in the story. The only tragic death was a Swedish farmer who was visiting the town and did not understand the robbers who were yelling at him to get off the street, and he was shot and killed.

Joseph L. Haywood was born in Fitzwilliam, New Hampshire on August 12, 1837. His father was a farmer, a member of the Republican Party and one of the leading New England opponents of slavery. Young Haywood served in the Union army, took part in the Battle of Vicksburg and later on, because of health reasons, he was transferred to Nashville, Tennessee where he worked at a local hospital. He was discharged from the army in 1865 and in 1867 he arrived in Northfield where he worked as a bookkeeper at a sawmill owned by S. P. Stewart. He became an accountant of the First National Bank in 1872 and when needed he also carried out the duty of a treasurer. On the day of the robbery he substituted for the chief treasurer who was on vacation. Who actually shot him was never established beyond any doubt. It was generally believed it was Jesse who had the reputation of a cold blooded killer, but other historians such as Mark Lee Gardner are convinced that it was his brother Frank while Jesse was participating in the shootout outside the bank. Shortly after Haywood's death, a special fund was set up for the widow in the amount of $12,602 to which banks practically from all states of the Union contributed. Haywood did not only work for the Northfield bank but he was also the treasurer of the local university (**Carleton College**) and eventually a special commemorative plaque was unveiled in the university library. In **The First Congregational Church** located in downtown Northfield a visitor can see Haywood's name with an inscription in memoriam inserted in one of the church windows. His body was buried at the local cemetery and the grave is well maintained to this day.

New Prague was founded by **Anton Filip** in 1856 as a center of the Czech settlers in the southern part of Minnesota. Even though the town is now fully Americanized, a nearby cemetery is a unique witness to the large wave of Czech immigrants from the second half of the nineteenth century. Several hundred graves carry not only Czech names, but also the inscriptions are in the Czech language. An interesting building is the Catholic church of St. Wenceslas. Dozhinkee (**dožinky**), a special Czech holiday celebrating the end of harvest, is still one of the most popular local events.